Dizzy Fantastic

and Her Flying Bicycle

by Andy Mueller

Bonneville Books
Springville, Utah

ISBN 13: 978-1-59955-395-5

Published by Bonneville Books, an imprint of Cedar Fort, Inc., 2373 W. 700 S., Springville, UT 84663

Distributed by Cedar Fort, Inc., www.cedarfort.com

LIBRARY OF CONGRESS CATALOGING-IN-PUBLICATION DATA

Hueller, Andy.
 Dizzy Fantastic and her flying bicycle / Andy Hueller.
   p. cm.
 Summary: Fourth-grader Debbie Fine has an adventurous summer when she imagines herself to be Dizzy Fantastic, a superhero who rides a flying bicycle.
 ISBN 978-1-59955-395-5 (acid-free paper)
 [1. Imagination--Fiction. 2. Superheroes--Fiction. 3.
Self-confidence--Fiction. 4. Interpersonal relations--Fiction. 5.
Vacations--Fiction.] I. Title.
 PZ7.H8694Diz 2010
 [Fic]--dc22

                              2010005521

Illustrations by Melissa Bastow
Cover design by Megan Whittier
Cover design © 2010 by Lyle Mortimer
Edited and typeset by Megan E. Welton

Printed in Canada

10 9 8 7 6 5 4 3 2 1

Printed on acid-free paper

★⋅★⋅★
To my wife, the real superhero.

⋅★⋅★⋅★

·.★ ONE ★·:

E asy, T-Rex. Easy, boy."
Debbie felt the dog's wet nose and hot breath on her calf, and she pushed down harder on her bike pedal. The canine beast growled behind her, his tags tinkling menacingly, his big paws thumping.

"Easy, T-Rex," Debbie said again. "Easy, boy."

But the slobbering dog kept after her.

All Debbie had going for her was her bike—the shining white Thunderstrike her parents had given her for her birthday over the summer. Since then, she'd gone everywhere on the bike. Up the hill to school five days a week. Over eighteen blocks to Cone On In! Ice Cream Parlor for a scoop of peppermint bon-bon and to say hello to her parents, who owned the little shop. Down (*thunk! thunk! thunk!*) Plaintown's tall, twisting, cement staircase. Past the Costellos' elaborate and trellised front garden—marvelous mysteries surely waiting inside. And past Mean Mr. Wilson's front curb on the way to school. Mr. Wilson had a sign out front that said, "THIS IS NOT YOUR LAWN. STAY OFF." Another sign, closer to the front porch, said, "PASS QUIETLY AT YOUR OWN RISK. DO NOT DISTURB THE ANGRY RED BEES." There was always a buzzing noise coming from the screened-in porch, and under the porch door there was a red glow. Of course, Mr. Wilson didn't need the signs or the bees; he had tethered T-Rex the Slobbering, Growling, Murderous Dog to the front step. Whenever Debbie rolled by, she would turn to read Mr. Wilson's strange signs. She couldn't help it. And that's when T-Rex would rise from his water bowl and pounce. The green rope connecting him to the front stoop would go taut and yank him back into the yard, away from the curb. Debbie thanked her lucky stars every day for the green rope that tethered T-Rex to the house and kept him away from her.

The tether had worked every day for as long as Debbie could remember. Until this afternoon. This afternoon, as Debbie rode by, T-Rex rose, pounced, and—*snap!*—the line broke. He bounded after her, looking to tackle and kill, like how the lions tackled the gazelles in that video the substitute teacher had shown them.

"Easy, boy." It was the only thing she could think to say.

All she could do was pedal—harder and harder. Debbie was four blocks from her house at the bottom of the hill. Usually she took her feet off the pedals, rested them on the frame of her bike, and glided down to her home. But usually she didn't have the town's biggest dog slobbering after her, fangs bared.

So downhill she pedaled, willing her bike to go faster and faster. Soon she'd need to slow down to make the left turn onto her street, then another left into her driveway. By then, she would need to create enough distance between her and T-Rex so that she could get off her bike and sprint into her house before he caught and devoured her. She thought again of the lions from the video. Those poor gazelles.

She flew by the Costellos' garden on her left. She was almost home.

She pedaled harder. She was going faster than ever before.

She looked behind her and saw T-Rex inches from her bike's back wheel, claws and fangs leading the way. Debbie whipped her head around and burrowed her forehead into her Thunderstrike's pink handlebar cushion. "Faster," she said. "Come on—*faster!*" She felt the great strain on her calves and hamstrings but kept pedaling.

She somehow pushed down even harder on the pedals. Faster and faster her Thunderstrike bike went, with Debbie pedaling with all her might.

When she looked back up, she was, to her great horror, heading straight for the curb at the bottom of the hill. Debbie had overshot her house and was only moments away from crashing into her across-the-street neighbor's front door!

She was going so fast, trying to stop her bike would have been pointless. Not that she'd want to with T-Rex right behind her. She didn't know what to do, so she closed her eyes and kept pedaling. It's what felt right. If she was going to die today, splatting into the neighbor's house was a better option than being torn apart by a rabid dog.

She kept pedaling, pedaling, pedaling. She didn't dare open her eyes.

Ten seconds later, still pedaling, she thought, *Shouldn't I have hit the house by now? Shouldn't I be, like, dead?* She cracked one eye open—and she didn't see a house. Instead, she saw blue. Nothing but blue.

She opened up her other eye. More blue. Confused, she looked behind her. Even more blue.

She looked down. There, she saw the roof of her

house on the corner. And across the street was the roof of the neighbor's house she should have run into. And in front of the neighbor's house, way down below, was T-Rex. He was small down there, but she could see that he was jumping up and down. She thought she heard his faint barking.

Debbie Fine, fourth grader, had flown on a flying bicycle over the neighbor's house.

⋅⋆★ TWO ★⋆⋆

An hour later, Debbie was sitting in her bedroom. She was trying sunglasses and capes she'd cut out of old T-shirts on one of her Barbies. "Dangerous Debbie," she said. "Debbie Danger. Danger Girl. Biker Girl. Miss Thunderstrike. The Flying Cyclist."

Debbie just couldn't think of a good superhero name for herself. Truthfully, she didn't even know if she was a superhero. What did it take to be a superhero? Did having a flying bike make her one?

She decided she'd better consult an expert.

★⋆★⋆★⋆

Her older brother's room was the next door down. Debbie heard noise coming from inside. Music and people talking. She pushed the door open and found James sitting in an armchair. Only his curly hair could be seen over the back of the armchair.

"Mmm," her brother moaned. He was in sixth grade,

two grades ahead of her, and he was always too busy to talk to her.

"James, can I come in?"

"Mmm," he moaned again.

Over the armchair, Debbie could see a movie playing on the black-and-white TV against the back wall. It could have been *Spider-Man* or *Spider-Man 2*. Debbie had never paid close enough attention when they watched movies with her parents. On movie nights in the Fine household, she always dragged the Barbie house her grandfather built for her mother out to the family room and kept busy staging scenarios: Barbie's friends coming over for dance parties or the whole gang hanging out in the pool, which was a small wooden drawer Debbie filled at the kitchen faucet. Sitting in her family's cramped living room, she couldn't help feeling a bit jealous of Barbie, her many friends, and her luxurious mansion with a pool.

"James, I have a question," Debbie said, entering his bedroom.

James didn't acknowledge her at first. She tried to wait patiently. She watched him glance up at the TV and then return his attention to the comic book he held in front of him. Debbie saw pictures of gray and blue and yellow and maroon costumed characters punching and jumping and kicking in the pages of her brother's comic book. She recognized the music now too: It was the *Superman* soundtrack he'd gotten for his birthday when she got her bike. Neither of their birthdays were actually in the summer—his was in September, hers in February—but their parents hadn't had the money to buy them presents in the fall or winter. Business at the ice cream shop was always a little better in the summer, so that's when James and Debbie got their birthday presents.

"James!" she tried again. This time he turned around.

"Whattaya want, Debbie?"

Debbie composed herself. Her question might give James a heart attack. "I want to know, like, what a superhero is. I mean, what makes someone a superhero?"

Five full seconds of silence.

Finally: "What do you care?" James asked.

"I—I just do, okay? So can you tell me?"

James kept reading his comic book. Debbie didn't understand how he could do this—watch and read and talk and listen to music at the same time. By now he had a lot of practice, at least. This was how their conversations in his room always went. Now he said, "Fine. A superhero is someone who can do out of the ordinary things. You know, like fly—"

"Fly?" Debbie muttered. "I thought so."

"Yeah, fly. Or breathe under water or be in more than one place at the same time."

Kind of like Mom, Debbie thought. *That's what everyone's always saying about her. That she's in a thousand places at the same time—working with Dad at the shop, bringing James to Brad Bemon's house, cooking dinner—*

"Plus, a superhero's got to protect some people or some place," James continued, "like a city."

Debbie didn't know who she could ever protect. Her Barbies? She thought she'd better change the subject. "Well, what's a good name for a superhero?"

"There's lots of them." His attention dropped to the comic book. "Wolverine, Cyclops, Dr. X." He looked up at the movie playing on his black-and-white TV. "Spider-Man. Superman. Anything with 'man' in it seems to work."

"So what if I was a superhero? What would you call me?"

"What?" James asked.

"What would you call me if I was a superhero?"

"You could never be a superhero."

"Why not?"

"First off," James said, facing the TV as Spider-Man swooped low, swinging on a web, "you're only in fourth grade. And you're a girl."

"There aren't any girl superheroes?"

"Only lame ones. Now get out of here, Debbie. All of your questions are making me dizzy." Without looking away from his comic book, he snagged a pillow off his bed and chucked it over his shoulder at his sister. She stepped to the left as it flipped past her through the doorway and settled on the hallway carpet.

Dizzy? Debbie thought. *I like that. Dizzy.*

★.★ ★.★.★.★

Debbie plopped down on her bed and thought about what it had been like to fly that afternoon. She hadn't been up there long—just enough time to figure out that she could go faster by pedaling harder, turn using the handlebars, go up when she leaned back, and down when she leaned forward. After a minute or so of basking in the sun way up there and relishing the sight of T-Rex barking like mad, she'd angled her Thunderstrike bike down to her driveway, parked it in the garage, and run into her house before the rabid dog still across the street knew what had happened. A part of her wished now that she'd flown around a bit more, so she could really feel the exhilaration of defying gravity. But she'd been too afraid someone would see her and tell her to come down or scream or call her parents. And that wouldn't do. No— this was something she wanted to do on her own terms. That's what appealed to her about being a superhero: if she wore a costume, who she was would be her secret.

The last thing she wanted to do was tell anyone about flying high in the air on a bicycle. Not even Diana, her always well-dressed and forever popular imaginary twin sister. The school counselor, Tabby, told Debbie she'd hung onto Diana for too long. Debbie knew Tabby was right. School was hard without friends. No one ever said hi to her when she got to school. No one wanted to be her partner during activities or group projects. Not that she could blame them. She was always daydreaming in school, and she never knew what she was supposed to be doing. Some of her peers were meaner than others, though.

Tony Tompkins and Richie Riggles said she was chubby. Alexis Alden and Nicole Nelson made fun of her clothes, which usually came as gifts from her relatives. Her bangs, cut straight across by her mother, didn't help her fit in either. Alexis Alden and Nicole Nelson looked like Debbie's Barbies—thin, with form-fitting jeans, sparkly flat shoes, and trendy tops. They were the only fourth-graders who wore eyeliner and blush to school.

A knock on her bedroom door pulled Debbie from her thoughts. "James?" she called. Her brother rarely knocked before entering.

"It's me, sweetheart." Oh, it was her dad—home late, as usual. Most nights he stayed at Cone On In! well after closing going over the books, taking inventory, and preparing for the next day. Making a living as the owners of a small ice cream parlor would have been hard enough. And then Dairy Queen opened on the same block only four months after Cone On In! welcomed its first customers. By the time DQ announced it was moving in, the Fines had already bought their property, had nearly finished painting it, and certainly couldn't afford to shift plans. "I would have switched it to a tool shop," Debbie's dad liked to say. "Oh, Nuts! always appealed to me as a store name. Heck—that's what we call our praline pecan. But when it comes to fixing things, I can't tell a whatchamacallit from a thingamajig."

Still lying on her bed, Debbie said, "Come in, Dad."

Dennis Fine was a short, squat, round-shouldered man with tufts of hair on the sides of his head and none on top. Like his daughter, Debbie, he had wide feet. Really, all the Fines had the same build. They were healthy, active people, but they were also, according to Dennis, "soft and stout like marshmallows, and everybody loves marshmallows—Rocky Road is one of our most popular flavors." He often said that he in particular looked the way he did because he had the weight of the world—or at least a small business and a precious family—on his shoulders. And yet, in spite of the money problems he and his family faced, Dennis Fine always had a gleam in his eyes.

"Whatcha doing, sweetheart?" Debbie's dad asked her.

"I guess I was lost to the world again," she said.

"Ah, yes," her dad replied with a smile. "And how is the World According to Debbie these days?"

"Fine, Dad."

"Full of ponies and princesses and rainbows. That's what girls like these days, right?"

Debbie grinned at her father.

"All right, all right. I was just making the rounds to see if you and your brother were up for a game of Jenga with the family." Jenga was the Fine family's favorite game. "But I can tell you're busy. I'll just say hi and goodnight."

"You too."

Debbie's dad began to close the door and leave. Before closing it all the way, though, he popped his head in and said, "You're fantastic, Debbie. You know that?"

"Yeah, yeah, yeah," she replied.

After he left, though, the word wouldn't go away. *Fantastic*, Debbie thought. *Fantastic*. She looked down at her carpeted floor and saw her Barbie with the sunglasses and cape.

"Fantastic Debbie," she said, leaning off her bed and plucking the Barbie off the floor. "Debbie the Fantastic. Fantastic Dizzy," she added, remembering her brother's word.

And then she had it.

"From now on," she said, "they'll need to keep the skies clear for . . . for Dizzy Fantastic!"

✦✷✦ THREE ✦✷✦

Of course, nobody else would call her Dizzy Fantastic. Nobody else knew Dizzy Fantastic existed. In school, two boys had a different name for her.

"Chubby Debbie needs to go to the bathroom again," Richie Riggles taunted. Tony Tompkins laughed. She had raised her hand and asked for the hall pass. It was the fourth time she'd asked that morning.

"We know she's not going to put on any makeup," Alexis Alden said to Nicole Nelson. "I don't think she even knows what makeup is." The popular girls' faces were painted prettily, and they had matching shoulder-length haircuts.

"Yeah, but she really should change her clothes. What is that—a cow on her sweatshirt?" Nicole said. Nicole wore a stretchy purple v-necked shirt. Alexis's shirt was similar but blue.

"It's a moose," Debbie said, looking down at her sweatshirt and pointing to the illustration. "It has antlers."

The girls looked at each other and giggled.

"I like your shirts better than mine too," Debbie said. She felt bad after she said it. Her Aunt Laura had given her the moose sweatshirt.

"That's enough—all of you," said Ms. Pawn. "Of course you may have the hall pass, Debbie." She followed Debbie as she left the classroom. She said to her student in a low voice, "Is everything all right, dear? You've left the classroom on several occasions already."

"I—I'm fine, Ms. Pawn. I just need to use the bathroom." Debbie hated lying and almost never did it, but she didn't know what else to tell her teacher. Plus, it wasn't technically a lie. She really was going to the bathroom.

When Ms. Pawn closed the classroom door, Debbie walked to her locker to get her backpack. From there, she walked to the only girls bathroom on the floor, at the other end of the hall.

Once inside the bathroom, she pushed the heavy metal garbage can in front of the door. She went into the middle stall and took off her sweatshirt. Underneath, she was wearing her pink swimsuit. From her backpack, she took out her pink bike helmet, the pink-framed Barbie sunglasses she got in a Happy Meal, her pink winter boots with Velcro straps, and a white bed sheet with images of faded flowers all over. The sheet was an old faded one—the one she'd had in her crib as a baby. She put the sunglasses on first, jammed the bicycle helmet onto her head, and pulled her boots up over her socks and the cuffs of her jeans. Finally, she tied the bed sheet around her neck so that it fell over her shoulders and down her back. Before leaving the stall, Debbie listened to make sure no one was coming in. She opened the stall door and looked into the mirror over the sink in front of her.

"Dizzy Fantastic—the world's first fourth-grade superhero!" Debbie said, admiring the costume. She felt like a completely different person—strong, appreciated, and, of course, super.

"Is that really your costume?" someone asked her. Debbie almost jumped.

That's when she saw her in the mirror. She took off her sunglasses to get a better look.

"Oh, it's you," Debbie said, looking into the eyes of Diana, her imaginary twin sister. Diana looked, of course, just like Debbie. The same round face. The same freckles. The same brown hair. Diana, though, was wearing trendy jeans and a stylish pink top, *and* she had brushed her hair out of her face—no bangs cut by Mom hanging

over her forehead. She was thinner than Debbie too.

"It just seems so . . . so hand-me-down," Diana said. She was often critical of how Debbie dressed.

"It's the best I have," said Debbie. She closed her eyes and put her sunglasses back on. "You're not real anyways," she said.

When Debbie opened her eyes, Diana was gone, but Dizzy Fantastic was smiling back at her in the mirror, standing strong, her arms akimbo.

Debbie allowed herself to stare at Dizzy Fantastic for ten whole seconds and then went back into the stall, took off her boots, sunglasses, bike helmet, and cape. She pulled on her big cotton moose sweatshirt. She crammed her costume into her backpack, left the bathroom, and walked back toward her locker and Ms. Pawn's classroom.

For now, these brief encounters with Dizzy Fantastic would need to suffice. Debbie would have to wait until after school to try out flying again.

⋆.⋆ ★ FOUR ★⋆.⋆

After the final bell, Debbie rolled her white Thunderstrike bicycle to the back of the school. Standing against the building's brick wall so she couldn't be seen from the windows, she quickly changed into her Dizzy Fantastic costume. The teachers all should have been out front on bus duty, but she wanted to be careful. As Dizzy Fantastic, Debbie mounted her bike and rode it slowly and wobbly across the play field, nervous and excited about taking flight a second time.

Just then, she realized that she really didn't know how to make the bike fly. What had she done yesterday?

"Fly, bike," Debbie said lamely as she slowly wobbled along. "Fly."

Nothing happened.

"Come on," she said. "Fly now."

Still nothing.

She grew frustrated.

"What are you waiting for?" she asked her bicycle. As

she said this, she jerked up on the handlebars. The front wheel lifted off the ground, and Debbie lost her balance. She fell off the bike, landing painfully on her elbow. The bike landed on top of her.

She pushed the bike off of her, sat up, and glared at it. "If I can't even ride you without falling when you're on the ground, how am I going to fly on you again?" She felt ridiculous just then, sitting in the middle of a field with a sheet hanging from her neck, talking to her bicycle.

She took a deep breath to regain her composure. "What was I doing yesterday," she said to her bike, "that made you fly?"

It took a moment for her to put her finger on it. "Oh yeah! I was going fast. Really, really fast."

Debbie surveyed her surroundings. "How can I get going really, really fast?" she asked. She answered her own question: "I need to be going downhill. Yes, that's it, downhill."

And so Debbie wheeled her bike across the play field to what in the winter was the school's sledding hill. Up the hill she rolled her bike. Up and up and up. As she went up the tall hill, she questioned whether she'd really flown at all yesterday. It all seemed silly, now that she thought of it. Who ever heard of a flying bicycle? Perhaps her always overactive imagination, which had conjured for her a twin sister she knew wasn't real but couldn't quite get rid of, had fooled her again. And yet she pushed on, something telling her she needed to try.

At the top of the hill, she rolled the bike to the hard dirt path left in the hill's grass from all the wintertime sledding. Years ago, students had built a permanent jump out of more hard dirt at the bottom of the trail.

Once again, Dizzy Fantastic mounted her gleaming white Thunderstrike bicycle. "Here I go," she said to her bike. "Don't let me die, okay?" She let the slope of the hard-dirt trail pull her down a couple feet, and then she started pedaling. Soon she was up to a healthy speed and was still accelerating.

Pedaling like mad down the school's steepest hill, she reached missile-like speed. She concentrated on hitting the jump at the bottom of the hill. The jump looked bigger and bigger and scarier and scarier as her bike rushed her toward it. "This had better work," Dizzy Fantastic said, "or I'm a goner." She imagined herself flung forty feet, toppling again and again in the air before finally landing with a *crack!* on her head.

She closed her eyes as she reached the jump, leaving her life in fate's hands. She felt her bike swoop up the jump and then leave the earth altogether.

She kept pedaling, her eyes closed tight and her face squeezed into a grimace as she waited for the inevitable crash landing.

The crash never came. Dizzy Fantastic opened her eyes. She was climbing higher and higher into the air. She rose to the school building's first-floor windows, then the second-floor windows, and the third. When she rose above the building, she saw two buses departing on the other side. "If I go much higher, somebody's bound to see me," she said, knowing she wasn't ready for that yet. So she dropped her chin and pointed her bike down beneath the school building's roof line.

She pedaled harder and flew faster, creating wind that tossed her hair around in back and felt pleasant on her cheeks and neck. The wind whipped her cape up and taut; she heard it rippling wonderfully behind her. Dizzy Fantastic headed toward the small grove of trees on the school's outer boundaries. On her gleaming white Thunderstrike bicycle, she dove down into the dark grove filled with walnut trees where they played Capture the Flag in gym class. "No one will see me," she muttered.

Dizzy Fantastic, fourth-grade superhero, wove a messy pattern around and between trees, from one side of the valley to the other and then back again, zooming as close as she could to the trunks without touching them and picking up occasional scratches on her arms when she swooped too close to the branches.

"Whee!" she shouted.

Time got away from her as she whooshed around the trees, and when she finally emerged from the grove, it was almost dinner time.

★.★★.★

On her way home, gliding downhill, Debbie went by Mean Mr. Wilson's house. She couldn't help but turn and watch T-Rex strain against his tether. It must have been new, because it was black now instead of green. It was the same dog, though. T-Rex, the big black Labrador of death, was foaming at the mouth.

Something made Debbie want to stop and take a better look. She steered her bike to the other side of the street and came to a stop. Straddling her bicycle, she read Mr. Wilson's ominous signs. One that read "DO NOT DISTURB THE ANGRY RED BEES" grabbed her attention. She listened to the buzzing coming from the porch, and she focused for a moment on the glowing red light pouring out from underneath the porch door. *What are they*, she asked herself, *vampire bees? Do they drink human blood instead of nectar?*

That's when she heard his voice. "Hey, you," the raspy voice said. "I wanna talk to you."

Debbie saw Mean Mr. Wilson—greasy gray hair on his head, a scowl on his face—limp out the porch door. Not knowing what else to do, she sat down on her bicycle seat and pedaled quickly down the hill away from the mean old man to her family's small house on the corner. She didn't ride as fast as she had the previous afternoon. Mr. Wilson surely couldn't be as fast as his dog. But she didn't take her time, either. He was the one who fed T-Rex, after all.

⋆⋆★ FIVE ★⋆⋆

Debbie parked her bicycle in the garage next to the rusty brown racing bike that her brother and dad shared. Her dad had purchased the bike at a garage sale twenty-five years ago. He hadn't been able to afford a car then, but he'd needed to get to his parents' bakery and to the town's business college, where he took classes. The bike was still too big for James, who had trouble mounting it, but he made it work. He did this neat trick where, once he got the bike rolling straight, he'd pull his feet up and stand up on the bike like it was a skateboard. Debbie was always impressed. Still, she always felt guilty when she parked her new, expensive Thunderstrike next to the family's only other bike.

Debbie walked toward the front door of her family's home. Despite spending the afternoon zooming around on her bike, she wasn't tired. While riding for long stretches on the pavement tended to take a lot out of her, flying through the air apparently didn't require the same exertion. She felt like she could fly without losing much energy.

Debbie quickened her pace as she approached the front door. Her mom would be worried if she was late for dinner.

"Where is she?" she heard her brother scream. There was panic in his voice.

Since when does James care where I am? Debbie wondered as she pushed the front door open.

"Debbie—you're home," her mother said. "Just in time for Good Dinner." Good Dinner, as the Fine family called it, was a casserole Paula Fine made five nights a week. It wasn't anything special—noodles and marinara, sometimes with the grocery store's cheapest ground meat mixed in—but its title made it taste better. Feeding a family of four on the Fines' small and unpredictable income was difficult, and eating the same meal most nights helped Dennis and Paula budget their expenses.

"Hi, Mom. Is James worried about me?" Debbie couldn't help but feel proud.

James ran in then. "Debbie!" he said. "Have you seen The Flash?"

Oh, Debbie thought. *He's not worried about me; he's worried about his dumb rat.*

James's white rat was the family's only pet. It didn't cost much to sustain a rat, after all—just a few scraps of last night's Good Dinner.

"She's not in her cage," James said. "I must not have locked the door."

"I'm sure you'll find her, James," their mother assured him. "She's got to be around here somewhere. Where, after all, is she going to have it better than right here in this house? She eats better and has it easier than any of us."

"Where'd you look already?" Debbie asked. "Do you think she got outside?" Honestly, Debbie wasn't too disappointed. The little pet had never warmed to her. Every time she tried to hold her brother's rat, The Flash would skitter out of her hands and arms and bite Debbie's earlobes.

"Not unless you let her out when you came in," James said. "You better not have."

"I didn't let her out," Debbie replied. "I'm not stupid." She tried to nudge by her brother into the kitchen.

"Debbie—I mean, I know you're not stupid. I'm just—will you help me find her?"

"You want me to help you?" Debbie couldn't remember James ever asking for her help.

"Will you?" he pleaded.

"Okay. Fine. Where do you want to look first?"

★.·★.★.·

They decided they should spread out. James said he'd go outside because he hadn't looked there yet. He told Debbie to look around inside in case he missed something.

She started in the kitchen. *Maybe The Flash smelled dinner*, Debbie thought. She looked in all the drawers and cupboards. She peered behind the garbage bin. No rat in sight.

Next, Debbie looked in the home's one bathroom, which was small and had a shower but not a bathtub. No rat in there either.

She checked under the living room couch, which became her parents' bed every night. The Flash wasn't under there.

Debbie took a deep breath as she entered her brother's room. The floor was littered, as usual, with so many comic books and pieces of paper with his doodles on them that it would be hard to find anything, let alone a small white critter that scurried on the floor. Debbie picked up the comic books and pieces of paper one at a time and looked under each one. She checked under James's pillows and mattress too but couldn't find his rat.

Finally, Debbie went into her own tiny bedroom, hoping that she wouldn't find The Flash in there. She heard her mother on the kitchen phone with her dad: "Nope—hasn't found her yet, Dennis. Debbie's helping him now. He really shouldn't have called you at work. He was just so distraught. . . . No, I know you don't mind him or Debbie calling. Just wish you were too busy to take the call, I guess. Any customers since I left?"

Debbie was used to hearing her mom on the phone with her dad as he took his inventory. They worked together all day, but all they talked about then was the ice cream shop. In the evening, when most husbands and wives finally get a chance to relax and enjoy each other's company, Debbie's dad was at the shop and her mom was at home, preparing dinner and taking care of the house. By the time Dad got home, Mom was almost asleep on the pullout bed in the living room. So they did much of their evening talking over the phone—and even then they couldn't help but talk about business at Cone On In!

Debbie looked under her bed for James's pet rat. There were a couple Barbies there but nothing with a tail. Next Debbie checked her dresser drawers. The Flash wasn't there, either. She couldn't think of anywhere else to look, so she left her bedroom and went to the front door to find James.

★.★.★.★.•

All the way through Good Dinner, James was distraught. "What if Fred got her, Mom?" he said. Fred was the next-door neighbor's blaze-orange cat.

"I don't know what to tell you, James." Paula Fine ran her fingers through her short, thick hair. She didn't look as confident as she'd been before dinner that her son would find his pet. "Dad said he'd help look when he gets home."

Debbie didn't hear much of her brother and mother's conversation. She was busy thinking about her afternoon, flying through the trees at school. She'd never done anything so thrilling. So dangerous. So secret. She wondered where she should fly next, and her musing brought a smile to her face.

"You think this is funny, Debbie?" James accused. "How would you like it if one of your dumb Barbies ran away?"

Debbie stabbed at her casserole and felt bad that she hadn't found her brother's pet. She didn't know when he'd ever ask for her help again.

★.*★.★.*

After dinner, Debbie brushed her teeth and went to her bedroom. She changed into her pajamas and prepared to spend the next hour or so lost in her thoughts.

For Debbie, that meant putting her Barbies to bed. She swung the unpainted cedar front of her Barbie house open and picked up Skipper from the dinner table (where Debbie had placed her before going to dinner herself). She set Skipper in the second-floor bathroom first and helped her brush her teeth.

"I'm going to bed early, Mom," she called in her high-pitched Skipper voice to Skipper's Barbie mother. She picked up the Skipper doll and moved to drop her in her little bedroom down the Barbie house's third-floor hall. That's when a tail swished against her arm. Debbie looked into Skipper's bedroom, saw a white rat lying on her plastic doll's bed, and screamed at the top of her lungs: "James!"

Dizzy Fantastic had saved the day, and she hadn't even needed her flying bicycle.

˙·★★SIX★★˙·

They were in the cafeteria for lunch.

"Chubby Debbie has scratches on her neck," Richie Riggles said to Tony Tompkins. "Did you fight a cat for its food?" he asked her.

"I . . . ." Debbie didn't know what to say. She knew she couldn't say she'd been scratched by tree branches as she whizzed around on her flying bicycle. And she never had been a good liar. "I don't remember," she said.

The boys walked smirking to another table.

Debbie sat alone.

Then Richie turned around and came back. In a loud voice that grabbed the attention of every student in the cafeteria, he said, "Is there anything you won't eat, Chubby Debbie?" He leaned over and took off one of his dirty sneakers. He placed it on top of the table in front of her, smooshing her grape-jelly sandwich. "How about sneakers? Do you eat them too?" He glanced around the cafeteria before announcing, "I bet she slurps the laces like spaghetti noodles."

"Maybe she ate all her nice clothes," Debbie heard Nicole Nelson say to Alexis Alden.

Debbie looked down at the table. She never knew what to say or do when they started picking on her. She looked back up at Richie and shrugged.

He pushed his shoe down, flattening Debbie's sandwich. Then he grabbed the shoe and put it back on his foot.

Debbie dropped her gaze to the table. She wished Diana was with her right then. She sat uncomfortably, wanting Richie to go sit down, wanting her twin sister sitting next to her, sharing the attention. Her eyes closed, Debbie heard Diana appear on cue. She said to Richie, "Maybe she's chubby"—Diana never completely let Debbie off the hook—"but at least she doesn't smell like wet dog." Debbie almost grinned before she remembered that Diana wasn't real.

She heard Richie laugh above her, but by the time she opened her eyes, she was sitting by herself again. Some of the students were still staring at her.

That's when she felt her swimsuit straps scratching her shoulders beneath her clothes, and Debbie realized something.

She wasn't alone.

Dizzy Fantastic was right there with her. Dizzy Fantastic, who could fly through the air on a bicycle and who could rescue James's missing rat. She could do things that would impress people. She could do things that would make people glad she was around.

Dizzy Fantastic's presence gave Debbie strength the rest of the day. It didn't hurt as much as it should have when she returned to Ms. Pawn's classroom without her materials and Tony said, "What? Did she eat her books too?"

⋆⋆★ SEVEN ★⋆⋆

At 2:00, Debbie left Ms. Pawn's classroom for her appointment with Tabby.

Tabby, the school counselor, was the only adult in the building who went by her first name. "It's important that we're equals," she would say. "And you know what? Tabatha's my formal name, and only my parents call me that, so I'm asking you to call me what my friends call me."

Debbie liked Tabby. She met with her to work on social skills—"to just check in and see how things are going," as Tabby put it. Debbie never felt more isolated, though, than at that minute every Monday and Wednesday when Ms. Pawn would interrupt her lesson to remind Debbie to make her way to the office.

Before entering the counselor's office, Debbie admired her door. The door was really something—every inch covered with student artwork. There were drawings of balloons and stars and rainbows. Debbie's favorite piece was a sign smack dab in the middle of the door that said "Tabbyville" in big cartoonish letters, no two letters the same color. She didn't know who had drawn the sign—it could have been a second-grader or even someone in her fourth-grade class—but it helped make the room behind the door more than an office. It was its own place, a far-off location within the school where you could talk to someone who would really listen. Debbie actually looked forward to her trips to Tabbyville, even if it meant she would be asked questions she didn't want to answer. The door to Tabbyville was open a crack as usual, and yet Debbie knocked.

"Push it open," came the familiar response.

Tabby looked up and smiled as Debbie entered.

"Hey, Debbie. Go ahead and roll a chair over here." Instead of traditional four-legged chairs, Tabby used plastic exercise balls. She sat on one exercise ball behind her desk, and two others rested across the room from her in the corners of the office. Debbie rolled one with both hands up to Tabby's desk.

She looked up at the counselor and admired the way her gold necklace and rings shone against her dark skin. Though it was fall now, Tabby wore a long red summer dress that exuded confidence. She reminded Debbie of singers like Mariah Carey and Whitney Houston, whom she liked to listen to on the radio in the kitchen. When she did, her brother always shook his head and said, "Turn off the girl music, will ya?"

Debbie waited for the counselor to begin asking questions.

"I see that Diana isn't with us today." Tabby motioned to the third exercise ball, still in a corner. Until recently, Debbie had rolled that one up to the desk too. That's where Diana, her imaginary twin sister, always sat. Last year, when Debbie was in third grade and the counselor was in her first year at Plymouth Point Elementary, Tabby had indulged Debbie by treating Diana as if she were real. Six weeks ago, the beginning of fourth grade, she'd recommended that Debbie let her imaginary twin sister go. That way, she could make an effort to focus on the students around her. Debbie knew Tabby was right; it was tough to come to school every day and not have anyone to talk to or work on projects with.

"So how has it been going without her?" Tabby asked.

Debbie shrugged. "Good, I guess."

"Yeah? Has she popped in for any visits this week?"

Debbie shrugged again. She shrugged a lot around Tabby. "I saw her yesterday and today."

"And how did that feel, having her around?"

Debbie thought about it. "Like I don't need her," she finally said.

Tabby grinned a small grin. "Tell me more about that, Debbie."

"I—I don't know. I just—like you said, she's not real."

"How about you and making friends here at school? Any prospects? Have a conversation with anyone?"

Debbie shrugged. "Not really."

"No? Nothing exciting to report?"

"I've been thinking a lot about painting my Barbie house." She regretted saying it immediately. It was true—she had been thinking about it—but she hadn't been trying to. The only thing keeping her Barbie house from being perfect was that her grandpa had never painted it. The walls in all the rooms were the color of the cedar wood with which the house had been built. Weeks ago, she'd decided she would paint it. It would take a lot of work, but she looked forward to all the time she'd spend in her room with her Barbies. When she mentioned the idea to Tabby, though, the counselor had encouraged her to focus her energy on other things for now. Things she could do with kids in her class.

"I think that would be fun, Debbie. But I'm more concerned right now with your relationships here at school. You need to trust me: When you're open to it, friendship will find you. I know you love playing with your Barbies at home. The lives you give them, the fun things they do, the parties they attend—well, I'd love being around them too. Just remember that they can't experience life with you. They experience life through you. They don't feel or care or look out for you. There's no reciprocation there. No give and take. Human relationships are all about reciprocation—how we can help each other understand and appreciate this world. See the difference?"

Again, Debbie shrugged. "I think so," she said.

Tabby smiled. "Okay. Enough lecture for one afternoon, huh? Anything exciting happen this week?"

Yes! I flew on a bicycle! Debbie thought this but didn't say it. Instead, she said, "I found my brother James's pet rat, and he was happy I did."

"Well, good," said Tabby. "That's great to hear. A brother's approval always means a lot. I know I always tried to please my older brothers too. Still do, as a matter of fact. Now let me ask: Has anyone complimented you recently?"

Debbie knew this meant the meeting was almost over. Tabby always ended their meetings with a compliment. She said there were so many good things about Debbie, it was tough for her to choose just one. Sometimes she mentioned Debbie's creativity and limitless imagination, her kindness to others, or her respectful relationship with her parents.

Debbie shrugged. "My dad," she mumbled. "He said—I guess he said I'm fantastic." She smiled, seeing herself high up in the air on her bike, sunglasses glinting in the sun, cape flapping in the breeze. She wasn't just fantastic; she was Dizzy Fantastic.

"He's right," Tabby said. "You are. And I've got one for you too: you're the best shrugger around, Miss Debbie. No one can say more than you do just by lifting those shoulders a few inches."

Debbie couldn't help grinning. Tabby knew her, all right.

·.·★ EIGHT ★·:

After school, Debbie returned to the hill behind the building. She pedaled furiously down the hard-dirt sledding trail until the jump at the bottom flung her into the air. Once up in the sky, she pedaled over to the grove of trees. She dove down into it and zoomed amid the branches and leaves.

This time, she'd come prepared. From her jeans pockets she pulled rocks and green walnuts, one at a time, and threw them at targets she imagined in the trees. At first the targets were entirely imaginary. She hit the Joker from that scary Batman movie square in his smiling face. She had learned about Adolf Hitler, that awful German murderer, and she sent a walnut whistling through the air until it exploded against his nose. She knocked the Wicked Witch of the West's pointy hat right off of her head. These were bad people, and she was protecting humanity by defeating them. That's what James had said—a superhero protects people. Debbie couldn't help it, though, when Tony Tompkins and Richie Riggles appeared sitting together on a tree branch, pointing and laughing. As she passed them on her flying Thunderstrike bicycle, she grabbed the branch and shook it, and the boys tumbled off to the ground below. They landed on Alexis Alden and Nicole Nelson, who had been standing below, whispering insults. Debbie knew she'd feel guilty later. Her classmates were mean to one another, but they hadn't done anything as bad as the Joker or Hitler. But right now, she was too busy to feel guilty. She was caught up in the exhilarating fun of it all.

In and out she whizzed. Up and down she darted. Dizzy Fantastic was beginning to master her superpower.

⋆⋆★NINE★⋆⋆

Debbie glided down the hill from her school to her home. She closed her eyes for three long seconds and breathed in the fresh early-evening air. Summer had seeped into fall and left the days warmer and muggier than October typically allowed, but tonight it was unmistakably autumn. The air was crisp but not cold, and Debbie loved the way it cooled her skin and refreshed her mind.

Dizzy Fantastic had flown again, and oh what a flight it had been. Debbie felt on top of the world—confident, strong, ready to take on any challenge.

"Hey—I wanna talk to you," a raspy voice bellowed.

Debbie opened her eyes and saw, standing tall in front of her, Mean Mr. Wilson. She could either run him over or stop her bike, and instinctively she chose to stop, pulling hard on the handle brakes. She forced her bike to stop too suddenly, though, and it tipped over and skidded sideways. She could feel the gravel grab and tear the skin of her legs through her jeans. When she looked up, Mr. Wilson was bent over, picking up her bike. He dropped it against his curb.

"Stand up so we can talk," he ordered.

Debbie did what he asked. From the corner of her eye, she saw T-Rex straining against his tether.

"Now—are you the one's been harassing my dog?"

Debbie stammered, "Me? Ha—harassing T-Rex?"

"Two days ago, I'm out back and I hear a crack. I come out here to the front and I see my tether's snapped. And there you are, speeding away from here like you'd egged my house." He thought for a second. "Was that you too during homecoming week last year? Thought it was some teenager out for a good time, but now I'm not so sure. Anyway, two days ago? I went back inside to call the police. Then I thought I better get your side of it all, us being neighbors. I tried to talk to you yesterday, and off you went again on that bike. Awfully suspicious if you ask me."

Debbie looked up at Mean Mr. Wilson. His hair was grayer and greasier up close, and his chin was covered with gray, stubbly whiskers. He wore glasses with black frames that gave his face a permanently stern expression. Debbie knew she should say something, but she was too scared to think of anything.

"Got nothing to say, huh? Well, I'm running out of patience. That tether cost me $30. Way I figure it, you got to pay me back. Got any ideas?"

How could Debbie pay him back? She didn't have any money, and she knew she couldn't ask her parents for it. She'd heard them talking in hushed voices about how difficult it would be to pay the bills this month.

"No—didn't think so. So I came up with one. Here's what you're going to do, girl. You're going to help me tame my bees."

Debbie swallowed hard. "Your—your red bees, Mr. Wilson?" She pointed at the sign.

"No, not my red bees. My *angry* red bees. If you're going to point at a sign, you may as well read it properly."

Debbie cleared her throat. "How—I mean, how do you tame bees?"

"Well that, girl, is what I'm about to show you. Come on."

Debbie stood there, paralyzed. She listened to the buzzing coming from inside the porch. Her eyes fixated on the red glow under the porch door. Tabby had encouraged her to make connections with real people, but Debbie was sure this wasn't what she meant. Nobody in their right mind would be Mean Mr. Wilson's friend. It was too dangerous. The man kept thousands of vampire bees for pets. No—Debbie wasn't going in that porch. Not a chance. He couldn't make her.

Mr. Wilson glared down at her. "Seems you're having trouble finding the motivation. Suppose my broken tether isn't enough. Maybe I can help you find the courage." He picked up her white Thunderstrike bike—*That's Dizzy Fantastic's flying bicycle!* Debbie thought—and dragged it into the middle of the yard. "Help me tame these bees right now. All's I need is an extra set of hands, and you probably won't die unless you're allergic." She didn't know if she was or not. "Or, if you run for it, I'll let T-Rex protect this bike in this yard for as long as he sees fit."

Debbie watched the mean old man drag her bike away. For a moment, she saw Dizzy Fantastic on top of it, being pulled from her along with her bike. Debbie couldn't stop her voice as it rose from her throat. "I'll do it," she murmured.

"Thought you'd reconsider. That's a special bike there, isn't it?" Mr. Wilson narrowed his eyes as he said this. "All right then—follow me."

Debbie took a step toward the curb and T-Rex jumped

for her. His wet nose touched her nose before the tether yanked him back into the yard.

"Easy boy," Mr. Wilson said, pointing to the ground. T-Rex sat.

Why does it work for him? Debbie thought. T-Rex growled as Debbie stepped onto Mr. Wilson's front lawn, but he obeyed his master.

When Mr. Wilson stepped up to his porch door, the toes of his black shoes glowed red as the light spilled out from under the door. The buzzing got louder and louder the closer to the porch Debbie stepped.

For the second time, she thought hard about making a run for it. But the thought of going on without Dizzy Fantastic and her flying bicycle was too much. She'd rather die a horrible death of bee stings than have to go on without her new courageous friend. Her new courageous self. Besides, she couldn't show up at home without the bicycle her parents had spent two years saving for.

When Mr. Wilson held the porch door open for her, she stepped in, closing her eyes but continuing to move forward. The buzzing now seemed to be on top of her, underneath her, all around her. She opened her eyes, refusing to let the bees take her without even seeing what they looked like.

"Relax, girl," Mr. Wilson said. "They're all in cans."

Sure enough, there wasn't a red bee in sight—just twenty-five Pringles cans lined up on the porch floor.

"There's an angry red bee in each one," said Mr. Wilson.

"Do—do they stay in the cans?" Debbie asked, feeling the faintest trace of relief fluttering through her body.

"No, they don't." Mr. Wilson seemed offended at the idea. "In the cans, they sit in one place." He narrowed his eyes again and focused on Debbie. "Angry red bees need to fly around or they lose the ability. You hear that? If they stop flying for too long, they may never fly again." His eyes widened again, though his scowl remained.

Was that true? Could a bee really lose its ability to fly if it sat around all day? She'd never heard that before, but she didn't know much about bees either.

When she didn't move, he said, "Girl, it's your job to open the lids and let them out. Go on now. Haven't got all day. Or you can turn back around and say good-bye to that flashy bike of yours."

Debbie stepped toward the Pringles cans. She wanted to look around the porch and see what else was in there, but she couldn't force her eyes away from the cans with the red bees. The buzzing was louder than ever as she bent over the cans. Slowly, slowly, slowly she picked up a can and looked through the plastic lid. The bottom of the lid had been covered with duct tape, and the holes that pierced the lid and the duct tape were too small for her to see anything.

"Open it up," she heard Mr. Wilson say behind her.

She held her breath as she peeled back the plastic lid and held the can away from her face. Nothing came out of the can.

"It must be sitting at the bottom still, girl. You better take a look."

Debbie brought the can closer and, with one eye closed, peered inside.

There, on the bottom of the can, written in red marker, was the letter B. Debbie heard Mr. Wilson's deep laugh behind her.

·.·★TEN★·.·

I'm sorry. I'm sorry. I'm sorry," Mr. Wilson said between laughs. It took him a while to collect himself enough to say anything else. "It's Debbie, right? Dennis Fine's girl. I'm sorry to scare you like that. Joke just doesn't work without fear."

Debbie looked around her for the first time. She saw a CD player in the corner of the porch and a small red heat lamp pointing at the porch door. Mr. Wilson got up and walked over to the CD player. He hit a button and a CD labeled *Buzzing Bees* rose out of the player. "You'll have to excuse my sense of humor, Debbie. Really, it was a joke for my grandkids. They liked it every time—though nothing beat the first time, of course, when they were really scared. But now they're all grown up with jobs and families. They've moved away. So the joke's become something to keep the teenagers and their toilet paper and eggs off my lawn. Not that it's worked," he grumbled, staring into space for a moment, but when he turned back to Debbie, he was smiling.

Debbie was still recovering. "But—" she started, and then stopped.

Mr. Wilson's eyes narrowed. "Do you have a question, Miss Fine?"

"Well—yeah, I guess I do."

"Shoot."

"Is there a B in every can," she asked, "or just in the closer ones?"

"Check for yourself."

She did. And sure enough, Mr. Wilson had written a B at the bottom of each. "Not really worth doing something if you're not going to go all the way, is it?" her neighbor asked.

Debbie shrugged. "I guess not."

"Now come on," Mr. Wilson said. "I want to officially introduce you to my dog. That's the real reason I stopped you. Couldn't help myself with the bees joke."

"To your dog, Mr. Wilson?" Debbie said, looking out at the drooling monster guarding her bike in the middle of Mr. Wilson's lawn. "I'm not sure that's such a good idea."

"That's because you don't know how to properly greet him. I'm going to show you. Just wait here a moment."

He went into his house, and Debbie thought again about getting out of there. She was beginning to trust her elderly, ornery neighbor, though, and plus—there was no wrestling her Thunderstrike bicycle from T-Rex. When Mr. Wilson returned, he carried two jars of peanut butter. He handed one to Debbie. Then he held his porch door open for her for a second time and said, "After you, Miss Fine."

Debbie walked down the porch steps and stopped, keeping her eyes on the beast who'd chased her down the hill between their houses two days earlier. He was lying down near her bike, and his front paws were pressing down on the lawn, his eyes on Debbie. Though he was resting, he looked ready to pounce.

Mr. Wilson said, "Excuse me, Miss Fine," and walked past her and right up to his dog, who stood to greet him. Mr. Wilson showed T-Rex the jar of peanut butter, and the dog sat down politely. The owner unscrewed the top and stuck two fingers deep into the gooey, chunky peanut butter. Debbie saw T-Rex's tail wagging impatiently. Mr. Wilson extended his fingers all the way to T-Rex's nose, and out came the big dog's long tongue. He licked and licked, lapping the peanut butter up. When it was all gone, he turned his head away from them and made smacking sounds as he worked the peanut butter from his mouth to his throat.

"See, Miss Fine? He's got good manners. He knows nobody likes watching someone eat with his mouth open. When he's finished smacking, it's your turn."

Debbie hoped T-Rex would never finish smacking. She jammed her hands into her pocket, hoping she'd never have to take them out again. That's when T-Rex looked up at her.

"Step right on up," Mr. Wilson said.

Debbie moved a bit closer to the dog, dug her fingers into the peanut butter jar Mr. Wilson had given her, and held them out for the dog to lick. She was still a good three feet from the dog's mouth, and she didn't plan on getting any closer.

Instead of waiting patiently as he had with Mr. Wilson, T-Rex stood up on four legs and barked at Debbie.

"Look," said Mr. Wilson. "Now you've offended him. You offered him Skippy peanut butter and he prefers Jif."

But you gave me this jar, Debbie thought.

"I'm joking, Miss Fine. Sorry—can't help myself. He'll eat anything. You're just not close enough. T-Rex doesn't like to reach for his food."

Taking a deep breath, Debbie inched closer to the dog. When she was right above him, he sat down again on his back legs and looked up into her face. Debbie cautiously placed her fingers right up to his nose, as Mr. Wilson had done, and let T-Rex lick the peanut butter off of them. His tongue tickled her fingers. When he'd removed all of the peanut butter, he turned his head like before and smacked away.

"A gentle giant, right?" Mr. Wilson asked.

"Right," Debbie said, amazed but not quite convinced yet. This was the same dog who'd been trying to devour her for years.

"Keep the peanut butter. That way, when you ride by each day, you can say hi properly."

"Thanks, Mr. Wilson," Debbie said as she unzipped her backpack—just enough to squeeze the jar of peanut butter in and not so much that Mr. Wilson could see her Dizzy Fantastic costume.

Mr. Wilson turned to walk into his porch. Debbie didn't move. "Is there anything else, Miss Fine?"

"Um, yeah," she said, peering around T-Rex's big back. "How do I get my bike?"

★ ELEVEN ★

Last night, Debbie had gotten home later than usual. Tonight, she was late for dinner. Her parents wouldn't be happy about it.

It was Good Dinner again, of course. Debbie could smell the marinara as she entered the Fine family's cramped little house.

"Debbie?" her mother called. "Is that you?"

"Yep—it's me," she said as she kicked off her shoes on the entryway mat. She dropped her backpack, and it hit the floor with a thud. She still had a couple handfuls of walnuts and rocks in there.

Her mother waited until she sat down to say anything else. "Where have you been? It's almost 6:30."

Debbie saw her dad sitting across from her. Now she felt even worse. He rarely made it home for dinner, and she regretted missing out on time with him.

"They almost called the cops," James said. "Since when is it okay to be late for family dinner?"

"It's not okay, James," said their mother. "Your sister has some explaining to do."

"I left Brad's house right before the water gun fight. It's not fair," said James. "I could have been with my friends for another hour instead of staring at cold food."

Debbie looked at the table and saw an untouched mound of casserole. Her family had waited for her to begin dinner.

"Easy," Dad said. "Let's let Debbie talk so we can eat."

"I—I'm sorry. I was talking with Mr. Wilson. We fed T-Rex."

"Mean Mr. Wilson?" James asked. "You're lying. Mom, Dad, tell Debbie she shouldn't tell lies at the dinner table."

"I'm sure Debbie's not lying, James," their father said.

Debbie smiled. She couldn't help herself. "I even met his red bees."

"His angry red bees?" her brother said, wide eyed.

Debbie nodded.

"Mr. Wilson's a very nice man," her dad said. "He's one of our most regular customers." Debbie and James both knew that at Cone On In! a regular customer might be someone who walked in once every month or two. "He likes our chocolate butterscotch swirl the best. And he always has something nice to say about this family. He often admires your lawn-mowing, son. Who knows—he may pay you to mow his lawn at some point. I mowed lawns for the neighbors when I was your age."

James shook his head. "Sorry, Dad. I'm not stepping foot on that grass."

"That's what I thought too," Debbie said, "but I was wrong. He's nice, like Dad said, and he's funny." Now that she thought about it, the angry red bee joke really was pretty good.

"I just wish you'd called," said Debbie's mother. "You're old enough to understand that people worry about you if they don't know where you are."

"I've missed you down at the shop these past few days, Debbie," her dad said. Since getting her bike, she had visited the shop once a day to say hi to her parents. "What have you been up to?"

Debbie wasn't sure how to respond. She'd been busy flying on her bicycle. "I—I've been learning tricks on the bike you and Mom got me. Like riding with no hands and pedaling down steep hills. I guess I'm getting pretty good."

"Nothing too dangerous?" her dad asked.

What did "too dangerous" mean? "I don't think so, Dad."

"Have you stood on the seat yet?" James asked.

Debbie shook her head.

"Of course not." Her brother looked pleased with himself. "Girls never do anything daring."

Debbie looked down at the table to conceal her grin. *Maybe Debbie Fine doesn't do anything daring, but Dizzy Fantastic darts in and out of trees on a flying bicycle*, she thought.

"Well why don't you come down to the shop sometime soon and show us your tricks?" her dad said. "Your mother and I would enjoy the company."

"Okay, Dad. I will."

"And then make sure you're home for dinner," her mom added.

✦.✦★ TWELVE ★✦.✦

After dinner, Debbie dragged her Barbie house into the living room. It was James's night to pick the movie. Since she preferred playing with her Barbies, he usually picked the movie. Tonight, he'd brought out *Superman Returns*. A year before, it had killed him not to see the movie in the theater, but Mr. and Mrs. Fine had already spent any leftover income on a few comic books for him and some Barbie clothes for Debbie. And James never took friends up on their offers to join their families at the movies. He didn't want to have to tell them he couldn't afford it. As usual when it came to small contributions, though, relatives had come through. They'd sent the DVD to him as an early Hanukkah gift. Debbie and James knew that small contributions, as their parents called holiday gifts, were always welcome, but never significant contributions. Uncle Lenny had once suggested that he pay July's electricity bill, and Debbie's and James's dad had politely asked him how he'd like it if they came over for dinner at his place and offered to replace his curtains. Debbie didn't really understand her dad's analogy, but she got the point.

Tonight, as James watched his movie, Debbie played out an exciting new scenario. She dressed up a Barbie as Dizzy Fantastic—sunglasses, boots, and a cape. All of her Ken dolls were present and well dressed, as were her Barbies. The Barbies were hosting a dance at their home. Her Barbies were in the ballroom, where all the dances happened. The ballroom was Debbie's favorite room in the house—though she thought that it, more than any other room, needed to be painted something bright and shiny. The unpainted cedar always felt too plain for the fancy get-togethers she put on in the space. And tonight, there would be more than dancing. Skipper was going to get hurt in some way—Debbie would have to improvise when she got there—and Dizzy Fantastic would swoop down in her flying convertible (Debbie didn't have a Barbie bicycle) and deliver Skipper to the hospital. Then the Barbies and Kens would spend the rest of the evening discussing how grateful they were for this superhero who came from out of nowhere to save the day.

"Who was she?" they'd ask.

"Where'd she come from?"

"At least we can always feel safe now, with Dizzy Fantastic looking out for us."

★⁝★★⋆⁝

Her Dizzy Fantastic doll put aside for now, Debbie set up one Barbie and Ken pair after another, matching colors as best she could. She could hear her parents snoring behind her. They usually fell asleep during the movie. They'd been up working since before 5:00 that morning, and now her mom's head rested on her dad's shoulder. Just then, something in James's movie caught Debbie's eye.

"What's he doing?" she thought aloud. Superman was floating face down above the clouds with his eyes shut.

"Shhh," James said. "I'm trying to watch the movie."

"Yeah—but what's he doing?"

"Superman's hovering above the Earth, listening for cries of help."

"Does that work?"

"Yeah, if you're from Krypton and you can hear people from way up there."

"Oh." Seeing Superman up there, Debbie realized that she had no idea how high Dizzy Fantastic could fly on her bicycle.

It was time she found out.

⋆⋆★ THIRTEEN ★⋆★

When the end-of-day school bell rang, Debbie had a schedule to follow. She would roll her bike to the top of the sledding hill, race down it, hit the jump at the bottom, and immediately pull her handle bars back and tilt her bicycle toward the clouds. She would fly as high as her white Thunderstrike bike would take her, and then she'd dive back down to the schoolyard, change clothes against the school building where nobody could see her, and ride on the ground to her parents' ice cream shop. That way, she'd please everybody—her parents and Dizzy Fantastic, who'd been itching under her sweatshirt all day to get out. In her mind, Ms. Pawn's cursive had become Dizzy Fantastic's loop de loops across the blackboard.

That day, Debbie had worn her gray sweatshirt with a drawing of Waldo from the *Where's Waldo?* books on the front. Her Aunt Janice had designed it for her with puff paint. There was a picture of Waldo's head, with his red-and-white cap, on the front. On the back, Aunt Janice had written "Where's Waldo?"

Today, Tony Tompkins had read the back of her sweatshirt out loud over and over, as he did every day she wore the sweatshirt: "Hey, Richie—where's Waldo?" Richie Riggles had responded, each time, with "Chubby Debbie ate him!"

Alexis Alden asked Nicole Nelson why, if Debbie could find Waldo, she couldn't find even one presentable outfit in her closet or dresser.

Every time their words began to hurt, Dizzy Fantastic's swimsuit strap tugged at Debbie's shoulder and reminded her of what was coming that afternoon.

★•★•★•

So here she was, rolling her bicycle up the sledding hill. And now she was mounting the bike. Next she was rushing down the hill at a tremendous clip, heading straight for the jump at the bottom. This was the first time she hadn't felt any fear—the first time she knew her bike wouldn't let her down.

Out and up the jump flung her. She leaned back, pulled her handlebars, tilted her front wheel, and ascended to the heavens. She peddled hard, wanting to travel fast enough that nobody would recognize her from below.

Dizzy Fantastic rose up to the tops of the tallest trees on the school grounds. She rose above them until there was nothing in her line of sight except blue fall sky, and she kept pedaling. "It's not tiring like riding up a hill," she said to herself.

She glanced down and saw her town. From way up in the sky, it looked like the crossword puzzles her grandmother filled in every morning—everything below was divided into squares. In one of the squares, she saw her school, and there was her house, five squares from school. Higher and higher she climbed.

"My parents' shop!" Debbie said, spotting the small building below. "I better get down there." But Dizzy Fantastic needed to satisfy her curiosity first—she needed to see how high her bike would take her. She kept pedaling.

When she reached a bright white cloud, she closed her eyes and pedaled right through it. It was cold and wet, and she emerged from the other side soaked to the skin and freezing. Water dripped off her bicycle's frame and wheels. "It's a good thing I wear a swimsuit for a costume," she said. It felt good to speak her thoughts out loud this high up in the air, where only she could hear them.

Pedaling became harder. "I guess my bike doesn't want to go any higher." It came to her, then, that it wasn't the bike; it was her. She remembered learning in school about the air thinning out as you went higher. Some people died trying to climb to the top of Mount Everest because they couldn't breathe as they neared the summit.

She felt satisfaction saying, "So this is as high as the great Dizzy Fantastic goes." After all, it was awfully high. Short of going to the moon, she didn't have real limits.

She pushed her handlebars level and then down. She pedaled through another cloud, remembering as she did what it had been like to run through the sprinkler in her cousin Amy's backyard on a gray and surprisingly cool morning that summer.

That's when she saw them—three men, dressed in black, wearing backpacks, falling toward the earth. Unlike her, though, they weren't riding flying bicycles. Debbie gasped. The next moment, two white parachutes exploded from the backpacks and expanded. "Oh, they're skydivers," she said, relieved. She knew this because her brother James had shown their parents pictures just last week and pleaded to go. They'd told him that legally, he needed to be eighteen, and they'd return to the conversation when he was. The parachutes yanked two of the men in black up as the third man continued to fall.

The third man's parachute didn't come out.

"What's he waiting for?" Dizzy Fantastic thought aloud. She heard, just then, a faint scream. "It . . . won't . . . open!" the whisper-scream said.

Debbie Fine might have been paralyzed with fear, but Dizzy Fantastic knew just what to do. She pointed her flying bicycle to a spot well below the falling man, and she pedaled furiously. She had to beat him to that spot.

Down, down the man in black fell, his arms flailing helplessly like broken wings.

Harder and harder Dizzy Fantastic pedaled, her cape rustling behind her. Down she dove. "Come on," she said through gritted teeth. "Need to get there first."

She did—just barely. She felt the falling man's weight on the back of her head and neck and shoulders, and she pulled back on her handle bars to tilt her bike up as she moved forward on her seat. The man's legs, unsupported, pulled his body down, and he sat down heavily behind her on her bicycle seat.

It had worked!

"What the—?" said the man behind her. Dizzy

Fantastic said, "Hold on" and tilted her flying bicycle down to the ground below. The extra weight pulled her Thunderstrike bicycle toward the earth faster than she was used to, but if she tugged gently on the handlebars and pedaled a bit harder, she could control the speed of the fall.

She brought them down easily to the grass. Her bike began to fall to the left, and she said with confidence, as if she saved falling men every day, "Put your feet on the ground." The man obeyed.

"Who—who are you?" he asked.

"Dizzy Fantastic, fourth-grade superhero," she said, pedaling her bike a yard or two away from the man.

"Where—where am I?" was his second question.

"This is my school. Now, if you'll excuse me, I need to get home for dinner." And with that, she rode off, leaving the man to rub his eyes and look up to the sky at his parachuting friends and the plane from which he'd jumped.

★FOURTEEN★

Debbie changed quickly on the other side of the school building. On her way home, she stopped at Mr. Wilson's curb.

T-Rex growled, straining against his tether.

"Easy, boy," Debbie said. She took off her backpack and removed from the front pocket the jar of Skippy peanut butter Mr. Wilson gave her the day before. She unscrewed the top and stuck two fingers into the gooey chunky peanut butter.

T-Rex was already sitting, his tail wagging impatiently.

Debbie held the peanut butter up to the big dog's nose, and he lapped it off with his wet, floppy tongue. It tickled, and she giggled.

When he turned his head to bashfully smack the peanut butter, she heard Mr. Wilson's laughter from the porch. "Wanna meet some angry red bees, Miss Fine?" he growled.

She looked up and watched the older man limp down a porch step. Today his scowl looked closer to a smile. Debbie saw that the gray color of his greasy, uncombed hair nearly matched the gray of his house. For the first time, neither the man nor his house was menacing.

Debbie shook her head, responding to her neighbor's question. "I need to go home for dinner, Mr. Wilson. Another time?"

"You got it. They're not going anywhere anytime soon."

✦✦ FIFTEEN ✦✦

I'm not late, am I?" Debbie called up to the kitchen from the entryway.

"Nope," her mother called back. "Did you make it to the shop today? Did you stop by after I left?"

"No. Sorry, Mom. Got caught up doing a new trick on my bike." She hadn't even had to lie!

Her mother poked her head out of the kitchen, looked Debbie in the eyes, and said, "Do stop by sometime soon, honey. Your father feels like he never gets to see you and James these days."

"I will, Mom." Indeed, part of Debbie's plea to her parents two years earlier when she first asked for her bike was that she would go everywhere on it—especially down to the shop in the summer and after school so her parents could spend more time with her. "How long until dinner's ready?"

"Ten minutes."

"Can I turn on the radio?"

"Sure, honey."

Debbie turned the knob to her favorite station and pushed the On button. Mariah Carey's "Dreamlover" flitted into the room.

"TURN OFF THE GIRL MUSIC!" her brother hollered from his bedroom. "I CAN HEAR IT FROM HERE."

Debbie sighed. "Can I go outside and wipe down my bike, then?"

"Just don't forget to wash your hands afterwards," her mother replied.

★⋆★⋆★

Regularly wiping down her bicycle with a damp rag was another part of Debbie's agreement with her parents. Actually, the three of them had sat down together to draft a contract for her to sign. Debbie had spotted the white Thunderstrike high up on a rack between a red Schwinn and a black Huffy when she wandered into Bob's Bikes downtown. She'd had this special, tingly feeling, like the bike was meant for her. The bicycle had appeared spotlighted by a particularly bright overhead light, the world had gone silent, and for a moment, nothing else had existed but Debbie and the gleaming white bike above. She'd sprinted down to her parents' ice cream shop two blocks away to tell them about it. They couldn't help acknowledge the excitement in her voice and eyes, but purchasing a bicycle wasn't something they could do every day. If her parents were going to find a way to save enough money to buy the bike, then Debbie had to prove she really wanted it—even almost-needed it. Her father had made clear that "all a person truly needs is her family and a roof to sleep under, but it's important that each person identifies those other things she almost-needs too." It took two years—twenty-six months, to be exact—but her parents got her the bicycle. Before they went down to Bob's to make the purchase, the three of them sat down again and reviewed the contract. Debbie signed the contract then, and she wasn't about to break it now, which meant, she knew, as she wiped the dirt off her front wheel, that she couldn't be late for dinner anymore, and she needed to visit her parents' shop soon.

★⁚★₊★⁚

Fifteen minutes later, after wiping down her bicycle, she washed her hands in the kitchen sink and then sat down at the table. Her mother passed her the bowl of Good Dinner and said, "Nice and shiny, Debbie?"

Debbie nodded.

"Debbie learned a new trick today on her bicycle," her mother said to James as he sat down for dinner.

James looked up from his plate and sized his sister up. "Have you stood on the seat yet?" he asked.

"No," she said. "But I've done some other cool stuff."

James shook his head. "Girls are such wimps," he said, stuffing a forkful of casserole into his mouth.

·.★SIXTEEN★·:

Debbie could hear Ms. Pawn's classroom before she got there. When she walked in, no one was sitting down. More than half of her classmates were holding *Plaintown Press* newspapers and pointing excitedly at the front page.

Kyle Knutsen came in behind her, a folded newspaper tucked under his arm. He spotted his friend Scott Samuels and said, "You saw it too!" Scott held up his newspaper and nodded, a big smile on his face.

Debbie didn't understand what was happening around her. All that came to mind was Ms. Pawn's current events assignment. Each morning, one student was required to bring in an article from the newspaper he thought was important. The student would then stand in front of the classroom, summarize the article, and explain why he thought it was relevant to all of their lives. Had Ms. Pawn moved the deadline for the assignment up to today? Had Debbie been daydreaming when the announcement was made? And why was everyone so happy about giving a presentation?

Maybe, Debbie thought, *I could read an article over somebody's shoulder and present on that.* She would probably only read half the article that way, with the second half being on another page in the middle of the newspaper, but at least she'd have something.

She peered over Kyle's shoulder and read the lead headline: SENATE DISCUSSING RENEWABLE ENERGY BILL. There was a close-up picture of two very serious looking men who wore glasses and were apparently thinking very hard about the bill. *But why does everybody in here care so much about that?* Debbie asked herself. And then she saw Kyle's finger point to a sentence in a different article, this one on the right side of the front page, in the bottom corner. Debbie's whole body tensed up, and she felt nervous sweat ooze from the pores all over her body. She read on, which was tough because Kyle kept moving his newspaper around as he talked enthusiastically with Scott. This is what she read:

SKYDIVER SAVED—BY 4th GRADE
SUPERHERO?

By Wendell Washington

Terry Tumble, 33, found himself in the middle of a

surprising predicament, a hard-to-believe resolution, and an unexpected place yesterday. First, he was falling through the air, hundreds of feet from the ground. This was not a surprise, as he'd accompanied two friends on a skydiving adventure. The shock came, however, when his parachute refused to open mid-fall. Now here's where things get hard to believe. According to Tumble, his fall was broken a hundred feet or so above the ground by someone on a bicycle—a flying bicycle, no less. This daring, unnaturally gifted rider allegedly brought Mr. Tumble to safety. The unexpected place of landing? A Plymouth Point Elementary play field. So who was this rider, seen wearing sunglasses and a bed sheet for a cape? "She said her name was Dizzy—Dizzy Fantastic, and that she was in fourth grade," recalled the stunned survivor, perhaps still fantastically dizzy himself. His friends, well above, confirmed that they saw something but weren't sure what.

So we leave it to you, faithful readers. Is there a Plymouth Point fourth-grader with the superpower of flight and a one-of-a-kind bike? Are Mr. Tumble and his pals pulling a fast one on us all? The readers of sound mind may tilt toward the latter, but do consider: the flight crew says three men jumped, and when they rounded the jumpers up, Tumble's parachute was stuck soundly in his pack. How did he get to the ground safely?

"Who do you think it is?" Debbie heard Kavitha Klemens ask. "If she's really in fourth grade, then she might be in our class!"

Debbie slipped to her desk and sat down. She

remembered how Superman rose above the Earth to listen in on conversations, and now Dizzy Fantastic would do the same from a school desk. She was the only one seated.

Students came up with lots of ideas. Owen Okibawe suggested that it was just an April Fool's joke. That theory gained momentum until Flora Flomstad reminded the class that it was October, not April. Mindy Mau said nobody in fourth grade could be a superhero. Maybe some short high schooler was the real superhero and just said she was in fourth grade to throw everybody off. Pete Pluck was certain that something else—like a lucky wind current or a big bird—had saved the falling man and then dropped him on his head, so now his memory was funny. Hillary Hopper said the skydivers were lying, and the people on the plane were in on the joke.

Richie Riggles was the only one to include Debbie in the discussion. He said to Tony Tompkins, "We know it's not Chubby Debbie. No bike could lift her off the ground. I bet her wheels go flat every time she sits down."

Debbie was thoroughly convinced, and relieved to know, that her superhero identity remained concealed.

And then someone tugged her elbow.

"Debbie Fine," that someone said, "I saw you. Out the window, I saw you."

★·★SEVENTEEN★·★

Debbie was fortunate. She hadn't known what to say that morning when Davey Cook told her he'd seen her. But she'd been saved from needing to say anything because Ms. Pawn had miraculously picked that very moment to ask everyone to sit down so they could officially begin school for the day. Debbie sat across the room from Davey so he couldn't talk to her about what he'd seen with others around. Every kid in school seemed to want to know more about Dizzy Fantastic.

Debbie still wasn't sure what to say to Davey when it was time for lunch, so she spent the period in a bathroom stall. At 2:30 in the afternoon, only half an hour before the end-of-day bell, she took a deep breath. She was feeling pretty good about her chances of leaving school that day without having to talk with Davey. That's when Ms. Pawn told the students to pair up and go for a walk-and-share around the classroom. Usually, the last student to find someone was stuck with Debbie, whom nobody chose. But this time, Davey made a beeline to Debbie. "Let's be partners," he said.

Debbie looked around, but everybody else was already pairing up. "Okay, we're partners," she conceded.

Davey Cook was about the same height as Debbie and skinnier than a meter stick. He sported an uneven bowl cut on the top of his head. He laughed repeatedly and loudly during silent reading (which meant he must have been really, really engrossed in what he was reading), he talked nonstop in the halls about box scores and injury reports with the other boys in class, and every day he wore sweatpants and a basketball jersey that went down to his knees.

Nicole Nelson saw Debbie and Davey standing together and said, "You two should start a modeling company. You could remind people what's definitely not in this season." Alexis Alden laughed.

Davey threw an eraser at them that just missed their noses. They scoffed and walked away.

"Uh—okay, so we learned something about long division," said Debbie, trying to stick to the assignment, hoping that if she didn't breathe, Davey wouldn't interrupt her. "And then we worked on those stories we're writing—"

"Yeah, that's right," Davey cut her off. "So anyway, Debbie—"

Deny, deny, deny, thought Debbie. No matter how sure he was that he'd seen her flying on her bicycle, she would say it wasn't her; he must be mistaken.

"Like I said, I, well, I saw you yesterday. And the day before too."

He'd seen her down in the trees behind the school? She'd thought she was safe there at least.

"My family lives near you. We're neighbors, I guess. Mom says you live on the corner, right? We, well, actually we live across the street from Mean Mr. Wilson. And I saw him make you go into his porch with all those angry red bees, and I thought I should call 911, but I didn't know what to tell them. I mean, nothing had happened yet. And then you came out, and you looked okay, and you stuck your fingers in T-Rex's mouth, and I was sure he ate your hand—like that was what you paid to keep your life or something." Davey's eyes got big as he remembered. "But then I saw you in school, and you had all your fingers, and you went back yesterday and did it again."

He didn't see Dizzy Fantastic flying! Debbie thought. *He just saw me at Mr. Wilson's.*

"So I was wondering," Davey continued. "How did you survive? Are you and Mr. Wilson, like, friends?"

"Um—yeah, kind of," she said. "I mean, I really only met him two days ago, when I guess you saw me go in his porch."

"Well, I don't get it. How do you get by T-Rex? And how big are those red bees?"

"Angry red bees," Debbie corrected him. "And I think you should ask Mr. Wilson, not me." She was pretty sure Mr. Wilson would love to play the joke again.

Davey thought about it. "I won't die?" he asked.

Debbie shook her head. "Probably not."

"Okay," he said. "Wanna go after school?"

"You want me to go with you?" Not one of her classmates had ever asked her to do something after school. "I—I'm supposed to go see my parents at their shop after school." She really wanted to take off again as Dizzy Fantastic—look at all the good she'd done yesterday!—but maybe it was better to lay low for a while, now that the newspaper had gotten everybody so curious. And she hadn't seen her dad much in a long time.

Davey looked disappointed. Despite his fear, he wanted to go to Mr. Wilson's. He wanted to go with her. Debbie remembered what Tabby had said—that she should try her hardest to make a connection with a real person in her class.

"I can go see my mom and dad tomorrow, though," she said. "Yeah, okay, let's go see Mr. Wilson today after school."

"Great." Davey took a deep breath. Either he wasn't sure he wanted to be spotted with Debbie after all, or he was imagining walking past T-Rex to Mr. Wilson's porch. "Meet you out front, then?"

"Sure."

As she turned to go back to her desk, Davey called, "Debbie?" *Here it is,* Debbie thought. *He's going to change his mind.*

"You're sure I'm not going to die, right?"

She smiled.

·.·★ EIGHTEEN ★·:

D ebbie watched Davey as she packed up her things. She was sure he'd bolt out of the classroom and leave her waiting out front. When Greg Gruber asked if he was up for some two-hand-touch, she knew Davey wouldn't pass up the better offer. When she walked out of the classroom, Davey said, "Just need to return Mr. Fudd's football. Meet you out there," and he took off down the hallway with the football under his arm. Debbie knew then that she should just go visit her parents and forget about the boy in her class who asked if she'd go with him somewhere.

Debbie unchained her white Thunderstrike bicycle, but she couldn't get herself to mount it and ride off. She had to at least see if somebody in her class would actually choose to spend the afternoon with her.

"He's not going to show," Debbie heard Diana say. "Let's just go home."

Debbie shut her eyes tight and said, "You don't know

that. And you're not real."

When she opened her eyes, Diana was nowhere in sight. But there was Davey Cook, jogging to her from the school's front doors.

★:★★★:

"So how long's your family lived there at the bottom of the hill?" Davey asked Debbie as the crossing guard stopped traffic for them. Davey didn't have his bike with him, so Debbie walked with him, holding onto her handlebars and rolling her bike between them.

"All my life," Debbie said. "My mom grew up in our house, and my dad moved in after they got married and Grandpa and Grandma moved to Florida." The conversation stopped there. It took Debbie a while to figure out that it was her turn to ask a question. "Um—how about you? I didn't know you lived across from Mr. Wilson."

"We moved in over the summer. Our old house was, well, old, and Dad says it would've cost as much to fix it as it did to buy this new one. Plus, the other house was too big for the four of us anyway—that's what Mom says. I don't know. It had these wood floors you could slide all the way across in your socks." He'd been talking quickly, and now he paused. His cheeks flushed. "Sorry—you don't want to hear this, do you?"

Debbie smiled at him. She didn't know what to say to this strange fast-talking boy.

Davey said, "Right. Okay. So my sister and me, we watched the Olympics together last winter. And, well, after the figure skating, we'd, you know, have our own competition. We'd judge each other. It was best to go first, though. That way, no matter how low she scored me, I could score her lower and win. You like skating—in the Olympics, I mean?"

"Oh, yeah!" Debbie said. "When we watched as a family, I brought my Barbies out and. . . ." It was Debbie's turn to reconsider. "You—you probably don't like Barbies, do you?"

His face reddened again. "No—I mean, kind of. I mean, my sister always made me play with her. She's older and she used to boss me around."

"Oh."

Davey looked at her. "It wasn't so bad, though, I guess."

Debbie grinned. She didn't know what else to say, and they walked the next block in silence.

★.★.★.

"You still want to do this?" Davey asked, taking a step back as T-Rex came to his feet and thumped toward them.

"Yeah, come on."

"Mr. Wilson," she called. "This is Davey Cook, and he wants to see your angry red bees."

"Girl—you back again?" came Mr. Wilson's response. "You think because you made it out unharmed the first time, it's gonna happen again?" He emerged from his front porch, greasy gray hair on his head and a scowl on his face. "Well," he said, limping up to them, "you're probably right. Angry red bees tend to take a liking to some, and it appears you're one of the lucky ones. This boy thinks he is too?"

Davey, wide eyed, didn't seem too sure. "No, well, that's not what I said," he stammered. He looked to Debbie for help.

"There's only one way to find out, boy," Mr. Wilson said, and he grabbed Davey's basketball jersey and tugged him down the walkway to the porch. "Easy, boy," he said to T-Rex, who barked viciously behind them. The dog lay down. As he flung open his porch door, Mr. Wilson turned to Debbie and winked.

★·★·★·

Mr. Wilson and Debbie laughed as Davey stood frozen in the middle of the porch, staring down at the letter B written in red on the bottom of a Pringles can.

They watched Davey's face as a widening smile brought color back to his cheeks. They chuckled as he looked up from the Pringles can and saw first the CD player—"So that's where the buzzing comes from," he mumbled—and then the heat lamp—"and that's why it's always red in here."

"Smart boy, your friend," Mr. Wilson said to Debbie.

My friend, Debbie repeated to herself. That wonderful word. The one Tabby kept asking her about. No, Davey wasn't a friend yet, but at least he wasn't made up.

"Ready to go meet T-Rex, Davey?" Mr. Wilson asked.

Davey didn't look convinced, but he said, "All right."

"You want to explain how it works, Miss Fine?"

She smiled at Mr. Wilson, nodded, and turned to Davey. "So you need a jar of peanut butter."

·.★NINETEEN★·

After Good Dinner, Debbie went to her room.
She set her Barbies all around the floor and tilted
their heads up. Then she took out three Ken dolls and,
with rubber bands and tissue paper, fastened makeshift
parachutes to their backs. She poked a hole in one of the
parachutes with a pencil.

The Barbies watched from below with terror in their
eyes as Debbie pushed the skydiving Kens off her bed.
It took a couple practice runs, but she finally got the
timing right. Just when all hope appeared lost for the Ken
with a hole in his parachute, her Dizzy Fantastic Barbie
swooped down in her flying convertible and broke his
fall. The Dizzy Fantastic Barbie delivered him safely to
his adoring and appreciative wife waiting for him on the
floor.

Debbie, lost in her imagination, hadn't realized what
she'd done until she played out the scenario several times.
The Ken doll with the hole in his parachute? Debbie had

cut off a part of Skipper's hair and glued it on top of the Ken's head.

She'd given him a bowl cut like Davey's.

When her dad, just home from work, poked his head in, he found his daughter laughing softly. "Lost as ever, Debbie?" he said with a broad smile.

"I was, Dad," she said. "But not so much anymore."

"Have a good day?"

"Yeah—a boy in my class lives near us. He wanted to meet Mr. Wilson, so I took him over there after school."

"That sounds nice. Why don't you bring him down to the shop too?"

"Maybe, Dad."

"But you're coming, right? Sooner than later?"

"Yeah, Dad. I'll be there."

⋆⋆★ TWENTY ★⋆⋆

At lunch the next day, as he left for recess with the other boys, Davey came up to Debbie, took off his backpack, unzipped it, and removed a plastic jar of chunky Jif peanut butter. "Now I'll always be ready," he said.

Debbie smiled.

In class that afternoon, Debbie wrote a good-bye letter to Diana. At the bottom of the letter, she wrote, "Thanks for being there—kind of. I guess I only almost-needed you. So long. We won't see each other ever again." She signed the letter and crumpled it up into a ball. On the way out of the room, she dropped it in the trash bin. She knew it was paper and should be recycled, but the trash bin felt more permanent.

Debbie Fine had never been happier. In one week, she had made three friends, if she counted the four-legged one who licked peanut butter off her fingers. She had flown on a flying white Thunderstrike bicycle around trees and above the clouds. She had even saved a man from certain death. Yes, she was feeling better, all right.

No—she wasn't feeling better—she was feeling invincible. No one could hurt her now.

"Ouch!" she said as Tony Tompkins stuck her in the side with the point of his pencil.

"Sorry, Chubby Debbie." To Richie Riggles, Tony said, "I wanted to see if she'd squeak like the Pillsbury Doughboy." Richie laughed.

"Tony Tompkins and Richie Riggles," Debbie said, turning on them and standing up tall. "Are you really that obsessed with me that you can't find anything better to do with your time? You must be madly in love with me." She raised her voice so everyone in the hall could hear. "No, I won't be your girlfriend, Tony. And I won't be yours, either, Richie."

"But—" Richie said.

"That's—that's not—" Tony stammered.

Debbie spun around, holding her head high, and marched down the hall and out the school's front doors. On her way down the hall, she heard her classmates say, "They *both* wanted to be her boyfriend?" "Can't they do anything on their own?"

Debbie kept walking. People she cared about wanted

to see her. And besides, it didn't matter what Richie or Tony or anyone else said.

She was Dizzy Fantastic. She was invincible.

⋆·⋆★TWENTY-ONE★⋆·⋆

D ebbie pulled up to Mr. Wilson's curb and laid her
bike down on his front lawn.

T-Rex rose to his full height and bounded for her,
but Debbie had the jar of peanut butter out before the
big bear of a black Lab was halfway there. He sat down,
his tail scraping the ground impatiently. She dipped her
fingers into the gooey, chunky peanut butter and held
them just above his nose.

She laughed, as always, as he licked her fingers clean.
When he lapped up all she had offered, he turned his
head and bashfully smacked away.

"Don't suppose anyone else wants to tame some angry
red bees, do they, Miss Fine?" Mr. Wilson limped down
the porch steps with a grin.

"No, Mr. Wilson. Just me."

"Well, that'll do just fine," he said. Debbie saw the corners
of his lips curl up toward his cheekbones. "I suppose you've
come to keep an old man company for a few minutes."

"If that's okay, Mr. Wilson."

He stepped onto the walkway that ran down the center of his lawn from the porch to the curb—and then he paused, one foot on the bottom step, the other on the walkway. A curious expression came over his face. His eyes narrowed and his lips closed. He grabbed his left forearm as if in pain. He looked at his arm with that curious expression on his face, as if he was surprised by the pain and didn't understand it. "Oh, no," he finally said. And then he toppled over onto the walkway.

"Mr. Wilson?" Debbie said. "Mr. Wilson?"

Now she screamed. "Mr. Wilson! Mr. Wilson! Are you okay?" She ran to him, getting down on her knees to see his face.

"Mr. Wilson! Say something."

His body was tense. He was pushing the ground with his hands, trying to get up, wheezing as he tried to breathe. His eyes fixed on Debbie, and through clenched teeth he said, "Don't forget about the angry red bees. And . . . and . . . take care of T-Rex for me."

The dog was next to him now, barking sharply as he pawed at Mr. Wilson's back. The man's eyes lost their focus then, his shoulders relaxed, and he exhaled a final time.

"No!" Debbie screamed. "No! I can help! I can help! I can help!"

Dizzy Fantastic knew she needed to get him on her bike. She would fly him to the hospital.

She grabbed Mr. Wilson's arm and pulled. He didn't budge. He was too heavy. She was in fourth grade, after all, and he was a full-grown man. "No," she said. "I can do this." Dizzy Fantastic wouldn't let him go. She pulled harder.

★⁚★.★⁚

When Davey Cook walked by, that's how he found them: Debbie Fine pulling on both of Mr. Wilson's arms, T-Rex barking and barking and barking.

"I'll call 911!" he said, running across the street and into his house.

★⁚★.★⁚

The ambulance arrived thirteen minutes later.

T-Rex was still barking over his owner.

Debbie was sitting next to them, her face buried in her arms. "I couldn't help him. I couldn't. I couldn't help him. I couldn't." She said it over and over.

Casey Wilson, eighty-three years old, had died of a heart attack.

✦.★TWENTY-TWO★✦

D ebbie didn't touch her food that night. Her brother had called down to the shop and told their parents what happened, and her parents had closed the shop early. Mrs. Fine even decided to fix tacos for dinner. "We need a change of pace," she said.

Tacos were Debbie's favorite, but tonight she didn't want to eat anything or talk to anyone. She wanted to make it all better. She wanted to fly Mr. Wilson to the hospital. She wanted to rescue him. That's what Dizzy Fantastic was supposed to do. During dinner, her father suggested that they make it a Jenga night. "It's been so long since we played as a family," he said.

Debbie shook her head.

She spent the evening in her room, replaying Mr. Wilson's fall in front of her Barbie house. Each time, Dizzy Fantastic would swoop in and fly a fallen Ken doll to the hospital, where the doctors announced he would make it.

Doing this felt good. And then Debbie remembered that it didn't change anything. In real life, Mr. Wilson was gone. In real life, Dizzy Fantastic couldn't save him, and neither could Debbie Fine.

She dove onto her bed and lay down, burying her face in her pillow.

She cried and cried. She cried until her face felt stiff and tired and hot, and she kept on crying. Her tears dampened her pillow, and she kept her eyes closed. She cried until her pillow was soaked through. Until her whole world was wet and sad. She wanted to feel the sadness and not see or hear or acknowledge anything or anyone around her.

At some point, Debbie's dad sat down next to her. He sat next to her quietly, occasionally clearing his throat. *How long has he been here*, Debbie wondered, *seconds or minutes?* She felt his hand gently rubbing her back. She heard his voice: "Do you want to talk about it, Debbie?"

She didn't answer. She couldn't. Talking would only break the spell. It would bring her back to the real world. All she wanted was to feel the sadness. To let it consume her.

Her dad stood up. She felt the mattress rise as the springs released his weight. From right next to her—or from the doorway, she wasn't sure—came his voice again: "Honey, if you need anything, your mom and me, we're here."

And then she was alone once more with her damp pillow and her stiff, hot, tired face. Alone once more with her sadness.

She'd made a friend, and now she'd lost him. *Is this what it's like to have friends, Tabby?* She yelled inside her head. *What do you know? I was better off before! I was. I was. Before Mr. Wilson. I was better off before. Before Tabby.*

Before Dizzy Fantastic.

✦ ✦ TWENTY-THREE ✦ ✦

Debbie woke up the next morning still wearing her pink swimsuit. It itched, and she took it off. She went to her dresser and dug through her drawers for something—what was that word Alexis Alden used? Oh, yes—something presentable.

First she grabbed her moose sweatshirt, then the one with Waldo on the front. She threw them over her shoulder, not caring where they landed. The next sweatshirt had a koala bear on it, and the next was covered with paw prints from animals of all different sizes, each print labeled—one from a vole, another from a lion, another from a mallard duck. These were the clothes her parents had found on clearance, the clothes her relatives had sent her because they knew she liked animals. She tossed these sweatshirts behind her and put on a faded gray T-shirt that was too small for her now. There was nothing in her room that Alexis Alden or Nicole Nelson would even think of wearing.

"Mom!" she yelled.

She stormed into the kitchen, where her mother was setting out bowls for oatmeal.

"Why don't I have anything presentable to wear to school?" she demanded. "All I've got are stupid sweatshirts that kids make fun of."

"Debbie—" began her mother.

"No, I mean it. Why can't you and Dad just get normal jobs so we can actually afford something? The only thing you ever gave me was a stupid bike I don't even want anymore."

"Debbie—" her mother tried again.

"Forget it! I don't want to go to school today."

"Okay," her mother said, looking her daughter right in the eyes. "You don't have to go."

★·★★·

Debbie hardly got out of bed that day or over the weekend.

She only left the house to feed T-Rex. She'd told the policemen that Mr. Wilson gave her the dog, and she promised to take care of him. She let him stay on his tether in Mr. Wilson's front yard during the day and in Mr. Wilson's living room at night.

T-Rex didn't rise and attack her when she walked up to him. He sat and stared at the front porch, whimpering. "I hear you, boy," Debbie said as she patted his head. And then she sat down next to him and whimpered too.

On Sunday, she went into Mr. Wilson's front porch and piled his CD player, his heat lamp, and his angry red bees Pringles cans into a big box. His secret was safe with her.

⋆·⋆ TWENTY-FOUR ⋆·⋆

D ebbie didn't go to school on Monday either. She went to Mr. Wilson's memorial service. Her parents closed the ice cream shop and accompanied her.

In the small church, Debbie saw Mr. Wilson's family—a son and a daughter, in their fifties, and four grandchildren in their twenties. The women wore dark dresses, the men collared shirts and ties. Each spoke from a podium. From them, Debbie learned that Mr. Wilson had taught high school science. He'd taken his kids and grandkids to baseball games when they still lived in town. He always kept score, and he always argued with the umpires. He'd lived the last eleven years alone, his wife having succumbed to cancer too early. He had a warm heart and a wry sense of humor.

Debbie already knew about his heart and sense of humor.

When the last grandchild had spoken and the pastor had finished his homily, the congregation walked in line down to the basement, where there were turkey sand-wiches. Fruit salad too. Lemonade to drink. A farewell marble cake for desert. Four photo albums had been left open on a table against the wall.

Debbie's parents took turns putting an arm around her. She leaned into them.

Davey Cook and his parents sat across from them with their food. Davey nodded to her, a small smile on his face. She nodded back.

★ː★.★ː

Mr. Wilson's son stopped her on her way out of the church.

"You're Debbie?" he asked.

"Yeah, I guess so," she said.

"Well—are you or aren't you? Why do you need to guess?" At first Debbie thought he was upset, and then she saw his lips curl up into that same small grin Mr. Wilson had had. "That's what Dad would have asked you, huh?"

He paused before continuing. "I understand he left T-Rex to you." He looked for confirmation in her eyes. "You two must have been close. He loved that dog."

"I . . . actually I only knew him for a few days."

"Well, you must have made quite an impression." Debbie saw mist in the man's eyes. "Thank you for being there for Dad. We wanted him to move closer to us, but I guess his home was here. He wasn't the moving type."

"You're welcome," Debbie said, looking straight up into the man's eyes. She saw Mr. Wilson again in his son's grin, and she thought she would begin crying all over.

TWENTY-FIVE

How about I give you a ride this morning, Debbie?" her father asked after breakfast.

She thought about it. "Thanks, Dad, but I want to make sure I stop by the shop today after school, and I don't want to have to walk home first to get my bike."

He smiled. "So today's the day, huh? The day I get to serve the smartest and prettiest girl in town a cone of ice cream?"

She smiled back. "Make it peppermint bon-bon."

"It's a deal."

★.:★.★.★:

Debbie couldn't concentrate at school. Ms. Pawn's voice sounded distant all morning, and the blackboard seemed miles away. Debbie stared vacantly at the blackboard as her mind took her elsewhere. She kept seeing Mr. Wilson fall, his son's small grin, T-Rex sitting in the front yard while watching Mr. Wilson's porch. There were too many moments and images to make sense of. She didn't want to make sense of them. Ms. Pawn had to walk to Debbie's desk after the lunch bell to ask if she was planning on going to the cafeteria.

In the afternoon, Debbie shoved Mr. Wilson out of her thoughts. For the rest of the day, her mind was blank. While she often daydreamed in class, this was different. It was as though her brain needed to regroup, as though it needed to figure out once again how to process what she saw and heard.

When all the students were asked to find partners, Ina Ilg was missing, and so there was an odd number. That meant, as usual, that Debbie was alone. Davey asked if she wanted to join him and Greg Gruber. "Let's all be partners," he suggested. She politely turned him down. She wanted to be alone.

★·★·★·★·

When school let out, Debbie felt the urge again to take flight on her Thunderstrike bicycle. A small voice inside her told her to roll her bike behind the school and up the sledding hill. But she didn't give in. She wasn't going to fly. Not today. Maybe not ever again. What point was there in being a superhero if you couldn't save the people you cared about? What was the point of wearing a cape and calling yourself a superhero if your friends could go and get hurt and you couldn't do anything about it, anyway? That's not what happened in James's movies, she was sure. She certainly wasn't a real superhero. She'd only been pretending, and it was better for everyone if she stayed firmly on the ground. No good would come of her whizzing around above town. Dizzy Fantastic had taken her away from her family. She'd made Debbie believe she was something she wasn't.

Her backpack did feel heavy, though, with those handfuls of rocks and walnuts at the bottom. But she could still carry the backpack, and she didn't want to get sidetracked returning the rocks and walnuts to the grove of trees and end up not going down to her parents' shop. Last week, things kept getting in the way. And she'd promised her dad that morning that she'd make it to the shop today.

✦·★ TWENTY-SIX ★✦

Knock, knock," Debbie said as she walked through Cone On In! Ice Cream Parlor's front door.

There were her parents, behind the glass counter. Her dad was wiping the top of the counter with a wet rag, and her mom was talking loudly on the phone with someone. "No—we didn't order six tubs of rainbow sherbet. I don't care what you have recorded in your computer, sir. We only ordered two—it's all we can pay for." Debbie knew her mother handled most of the business calls. "She's more assertive than I am," her dad would say. "Then again, that lamppost over there is more assertive than I am." Debbie smiled, thinking about it now. Her dad was right. He avoided confrontation at almost any cost. Please the customer was his motto. Problem was, he rarely had any customers.

Debbie's dad looked up now and saw his daughter walking to them. "Debbie, my girl!" he said. "One scoop of peppermint bon-bon, coming up."

Debbie watched him scoop up the green ice cream with chocolate chips and plop it into a sugar cone. "For the Princess of Plaintown," he said, handing the cone to her over the counter.

She licked all the way around the scoop of sweet, minty ice cream.

Her dad raised his eyebrows. "And?" he asked.

"It's delicious, Dad."

"Oh, great. Delicious is what I like to hear. Tell your friends. Word of mouth is the cheapest, most reliable advertising. At least that's what they taught me in business school."

"Dad?" Debbie said, hearing her mother still on the phone, arguing with some man many miles away. "I'm sorry I didn't come down here last week. I should have. Now I don't know what I was thinking."

Her attempt to be something she wasn't had been a mistake.

"I don't know about that," said her dad. He had a puzzled look on his face. His head was cocked to the side, his eyes were narrowed, and his eyebrows were closer together than they had been a moment before. "You got to meet a big dog and a nice neighbor, didn't you? That's got to count for something. But I am glad to see you."

"From now on, I'll be down here every afternoon," Debbie promised. "You can count on it."

Dennis Fine grinned, but his head was still cocked and his eyebrows were still close together. He was still puzzled.

★:★.★:

Debbie's father came home early again to have dinner with his family. After dinner, Debbie hurried to her room. She closed the door behind her.

On the carpeted floor, in the middle of the small bedroom, was her Dizzy Fantastic Barbie with the cape and sunglasses, sitting in the driver's seat of her pink convertible. Seeing the Barbie in the cape, rage rushed up and through Debbie. "Take off that stupid costume," she ordered. She took one quick step and kicked the car and the Barbie under her bed.

Her Barbie house was next to her, in front of her dresser. The front of the house was on hinges, and it was swung open now. Debbie looked the house over. Her grandpa had built the five-level home with solid cedar wood, and it looked as sturdy now as it did four years ago, when her mother had passed it on to her. There were six bedrooms, three bathrooms, a living room, a dining room, a kitchen, and of course the large ballroom on the lower level. The only thing missing, Debbie noticed once again, was color. The entire house was the natural color of the cedar wood with which it was built.

She made a decision right then. Once she'd made it, she couldn't keep the excitement inside her.

"I'm going to paint it," she exclaimed to the world. "I really am this time. And then we'll have the best and biggest bash ever!" All of her Barbies would be there. She'd make the place perfect for them.

She rifled through the art supplies drawer of her dresser until she found them: two strips of small paint compartments. She had yellow, blue, red, and white paint, and she could mix those colors to make other colors. She would spend as long as she needed right there in her room, far away from everything and everyone else, painting her Barbie house.

It could take weeks, she told herself. *Weeks of work here in my room!*

★TWENTY-SEVEN★

D ebbie's mother woke her up the next morning and encouraged her to leave for school early. She needed to feed T-Rex before homeroom.

She rode uphill to Mr. Wilson's curb and got off her bike there. She walked her bike up the walkway that ran through the middle of Mr. Wilson's yard. She leaned it against his front porch, went up the porch steps, and took out the set of keys the policeman had given her.

"Here I come, boy," she said through the closed door to T-Rex. She prepared to be bowled over by the big dog when she opened the front door. When she pushed the door open, though, and stepped into the tiny living room, she saw Mr. Wilson's black Lab lying down under the dining room table. He rested his head on his front paws. As she took a step closer, he pushed himself up onto all fours and slowly made his way to her.

"Good morning, boy," Debbie said. He stopped and looked up at her, and she patted his head. Then he lay back down, this time at her feet.

Debbie stepped over him and went through the house's dining room to the kitchen. On Mr. Wilson's refrigerator, she saw pictures of the family she'd met at the funeral—his children and grandchildren. She thought about how hard it must be for them—not having their father and grandfather around anymore. She could hardly even stand to be in his house, and she'd known him only for a few days. He had lived here, he was kind to her, and now he was gone. She hated the finality of it. It was all out of her control.

She kept moving, not wanting to think about it. At the back of the kitchen, on her left, was the door to the basement steps. She opened it and found T-Rex's giant bag of dog food on a ledge above the stairs. She picked up the bag with both hands and hauled it into the kitchen to T-Rex's bowl. She filled the bowl and returned the bag to the staircase ledge.

And then she realized.

This was the third day Debbie had fed T-Rex, once in the morning and once in the evening each day, and she was aware now that the bag was significantly lighter today than it had been the first day. And it was the only bag of kibble in the house.

How would her family ever feed him? Her family could barely afford to feed James's white rat. T-Rex's bag of kibble would be empty in maybe a week, and then what?

Debbie didn't want to think about it. The last time she'd mentioned money to her mom, Debbie had said things she regretted. Now Debbie tossed the thought about feeding T-Rex on top of a mounting pile of thoughts in a far, dark corner of her brain. A pile of thoughts she didn't want to think about.

T-Rex followed her out the front door, into the porch, and into the front yard. She tethered him there, and he promptly turned around, sat down, and stared back at the porch, where Mr. Wilson used to sit.

★TWENTY-EIGHT★

Debbie was thinking about what her Barbies would wear to the party when someone tapped her on the shoulder.

"Uh, Debbie?" Davey said. "You want to sit by us?" They were in the cafeteria, and Debbie was alone at her usual table. Davey pointed with his head to a table across the room. Greg Gruber was sitting over there with Henry Hill and some other boys. "Come on," Davey said.

She followed him to the table of boys. Davey sat down on an open bench, and Debbie sat next to him. "No—don't sit there!" Greg said. "Stand up!"

Of course. What was Debbie thinking? It didn't matter if Davey invited her—none of the other boys would want her sitting with them.

Debbie lifted herself off the bench and stammered, "Sorry. I mean—"

"You're sorry?" Greg had covered his face with his hand and he was looking at her through two of his fingers.

"What're you sorry about? You didn't put bologna on my seat."

"What?" asked Debbie.

"You, um, you should look at your pants. In the back."

Confused, Debbie followed Greg's instructions. She looked around her shoulder at the back of her pants. There, stuck to her backside, was a slice of bologna.

"I'm so sorry, Debbie. I put it there for Davey. It was a joke."

Davey crumpled up his lunch bag and threw it against his friend's head.

Debbie reached down and pealed the bologna off her jeans. "Is—is that mustard?" she asked.

Greg looked away. "Yeah—it's mustard, all right. I'm really sorry."

She didn't know what to do, so she looked down at Davey. He looked up at her with big, sympathetic eyes.

"I guess I better go clean this up," Debbie said. She dropped the bologna on her lunch tray and ran for the cafeteria doors.

She ran down the hall to the girls' bathroom, and there she wiped herself off as well as she could with paper towels.

She examined the stain in the mirror. *Maybe no one will notice,* she told herself.

Alexis Alden and Nicole Nelson were coming into the bathroom as she was leaving. Nicole looked down and saw the brownish yellow stain on Debbie's backside. She covered her mouth as she giggled and glanced at Alexis. Before the door swung shut, Debbie heard Nicole's voice: "I guess she forgot to pull down her pants first."

Then Alexis's voice, in reply: "I bet she'll still wear those pants to school again tomorrow." Both girls laughed.

★.★.★.·

That afternoon, Debbie walked as slowly as she could to Tabbyville. She wasn't looking forward to her visit. The school counselor would ask her about Mr. Wilson. Debbie knew her mother had called the counselor to explain what had happened. And Tabby would ask about Diana too. She always did. Debbie hadn't seen her imaginary twin sister since writing her that letter last week, but she would be embarrassed to admit to Tabby that she missed her. Diana hadn't always been nice, but she had always been reliable—always there, without needing to be asked. Debbie knew Tabby certainly wouldn't want to hear about the Barbie party she was planning or the house she was painting.

Halfway to Tabbyville, Debbie stopped, pivoted, and walked in the opposite direction to the nurse's office. She told the nurse she wasn't feeling very well and spent the final hour of school lying on a mattress, trying not to feel guilty about skipping her meeting.

⋅⋅★TWENTY-NINE★⋅

The rest of Debbie's week went pretty much the same as her first day back. She fed T-Rex from his diminishing bag of kibble, rode her bike to school, daydreamed through class, and sat alone at lunch. She didn't know whether Davey really wanted her to sit by him or not, but Greg had been avoiding eye contact with her ever since the bologna incident. Which worked just fine because Debbie didn't want to talk about it either.

She spent class time thinking about her Barbie house and the party she would throw once the house was painted.

★⋅★⋅★⋅

Except on Friday, that is. On Friday afternoon, Debbie thought about flying. No—not about flying. About not flying. In her daydream, again and again, she sped on her bicycle down the sledding hill behind the school. Each time she hit the jump at the bottom, she was flung out and up but then, instead of rising steadily to the clouds, she began to drop. No matter how hard and fast she pedaled in her mind, she fell. Before she hit the ground, the scene would begin again with her at the top of the sledding hill, picking up speed as she rolled down it. *Why can't I fly?* she found herself asking before reminding herself that she didn't want to fly anymore, anyway.

Debbie finally forced the scene out of her mind and went back to thinking about her Barbies.

★•★•★•

After school each day, Debbie rode her bike down to her parents' shop. Each day, something pulled at her; a small voice pleaded with her to roll her bike to the hill in back of the school and take flight. But she wouldn't give in. She tried to convince herself that the rocks and walnuts still in her backpack were not reminders of how exhilarating it had been to zoom through the trees. Instead, she insisted, the weight of them only comforted her; they reminded her that she'd be safe if she stayed on the ground where she belonged. She told herself this every afternoon as she pedaled her bike away from school to Cone On In! Ice Cream Parlor, where her parents served her a cone of peppermint bon-bon.

Her dad came home for dinner every evening that week.

After dinner, Debbie stayed up late into the night painting each room of her Barbie house. The bathroom now was a light pink with purple flowers, and Debbie drew each petal with a sharpened pencil before filling them all in with the paint. She drew the kitchen's tiled floor in pencil, and a protractor too, before flooding the squares with blue. Everything had to be just so. No detail could be missed. She couldn't afford one moment away from her room until she'd finished. She hadn't even started on the ballroom yet! This would be the party of the century—the biggest and best she'd ever thrown. By Friday night, she knew she would stay there all weekend decorating her Barbie house. She couldn't think of even one good reason to leave her bedroom.

It was her brother James's turn to save the day.

★:★.★:

"What are these, Debbie?" James asked Saturday afternoon.

"Oh, those," Debbie replied, glancing up at the mound of small bits of paper in her brother's hand. Each one said, You Are Invited. "Those are the invitations to the party."

"What party?"

"The one I'm throwing for my Barbies."

"Who are the invitations for, then?" He looked confused—or annoyed.

"Well, you know—my Barbies."

"Your plastic dolls need invitations?"

Debbie felt her face reddening. It did sound kind of silly when someone else said it. "How else are they going to know to come?" This sounded even sillier. She followed her brother's eyes to the Barbie house she was half-finished painting. He was definitely annoyed.

"Why do they need to know about it in advance?" he asked. "I mean, don't you just pick them up and put them in your Barbie house when you're ready to play?"

Debbie didn't know what to say.

"Anyway," James said, dropping the mound of invitations onto her dresser, "I was wondering if you want to listen to some music in my room."

He wants me to listen to his Superman *soundtrack with him?* Debbie wondered.

He waved a Mariah Carey CD case near his face so she could see what he had in mind. "I borrowed it from a girl at school," James said.

She followed her brother into his bedroom, and they sat on the floor between two tall stacks of comic books. They leaned their backs against his bed. James opened The Flash's cage, and she skittered up his arm and perched on his shoulder. He reached up behind him and hit the Play button on the CD player, which was sitting on his bed.

They didn't talk. They sat together and listened to "I'll Be There," "Hero," and "Make It Happen." The music made Debbie think of Tabby, who looked like a famous singer. She was still sorry she'd skipped their meeting. Tabby had always been nice to her. Even when no one else had.

Debbie leaned back against her brother's bed and sighed. It wasn't easy, having people in her life who really knew her and who counted on her. They had expectations for her, and she could let them down.

Mariah Carey sang the chorus, and her backup singers echoed it back.

Finally, her brother said, "Maybe girl music isn't so bad."

"Thanks, James," Debbie said.

They sat some more, in silence. Debbie closed her eyes

and let the music cover her like a warm blanket. With her brother next to her and Tabby out there somewhere in the music, Debbie felt safe enough to think about Mr. Wilson. It was the first time since the funeral that she'd allowed herself to remember his angry red bees. She thought of him throwing his head back and laughing as she stood staring into the empty Pringles can. She breathed in and out contentedly. It was a pleasant thought.

★.·★.★.·

Debbie never did make it back to her Barbie house. That evening, the Fine family played Jenga on the kitchen table. It had been a long time since they played last. "Too long," Debbie's dad said. "Way too long," Debbie's mom agreed. They played several rounds. They stacked the blocks higher and higher until the structure wobbled dangerously. Each time the tower of blocks fell, they built it back up together.

·.★THIRTY★.·

I n Ms. Pawn's classroom Monday, Debbie's not-flying daydream returned. This time, though, the jump at the bottom of the hill flung her only out and not up. She hurtled toward the ground, flailing, as her bike fell away from her. In her daydream, she'd lost the ability to fly even for a moment.

★·★.★·

After the final bell, she unlocked her bicycle's front wheel and rode up to the crosswalk. The school's crossing guard lifted the orange flags and walked to the center of the street, stopping traffic so she could get to the other side. She mounted her bike and glided down the three-block hill. Her house was at the bottom of the hill, but she wasn't stopping there. Eighteen blocks south of that was her destination: Cone On In! Ice Cream Parlor. As she pedaled, the small voice inside her suggested that she fly to her parents' shop, but Debbie was getting better at ignoring that voice.

She glided past the Costellos' mysterious garden on her left and Mary Rose the nanny's yellow house on her right. When she went by Mr. Wilson's front lawn, she hollered to T-Rex, still sitting and facing the front porch: "I'll be back with peanut butter and some dinner, boy." To her surprise, T-Rex turned his heavy head, rose up on all four legs, and bounded for her. He jumped as he reached the curb and—*snap!*—the black tether attached to his collar broke.

Debbie's first thought was, *I don't have any peanut butter ready!* But T-Rex didn't pounce. He didn't chase her. Instead, he jogged alongside her as she glided down the hill.

"Okay, boy," Debbie said. "You can come with me." She turned right at the bottom of the hill and rode away from her family's home. She predicted that T-Rex would get tired after a few blocks and either go back to Mr. Wilson's or slow his pace—but twelve blocks later, he was keeping up. Debbie said, "Good boy," and he looked up at her, his tongue dangling out of his mouth.

They passed Gus's Gasoline and Groceries on their right and, a block later, the fire station on the left. The police station was on the next block and across from it was the town library. Debbie curved left on her Thunderstrike and pedaled downtown, where the streets were bordered by bakeries and restaurants and bars and coffee shops.

When she hit Main Street, she hung a right, pedaling down the sidewalk past Vito's Italian Cuisine and Dairy Queen across the street. The sidewalk bent around a protruding bluff covered with trees displaying all the magnificent colors of autumn—reds and oranges and yellows. All this time, T-Rex stayed with her. *I haven't even offered him peanut butter,* Debbie thought.

And there, on the other side of the bluff, just before Main Street became Highway 7 and headed out of town, hidden from the view of most downtown visitors, was Cone On In! Ice Cream Parlor. Debbie felt proud every time she saw the small, squat brown building with the two-dimensional wooden ice cream cone on the roof. "There's just something about owning your own place," her father liked to say. "Nobody gets to tell you how to do your job when the business is yours to run."

Gliding up to her parents' shop, Debbie noticed that the door was flung open. *That's strange*, she thought. *They're always so careful to keep the energy bill down.* T-Rex growled beside her.

Debbie leaned her bike against the side of the building and walked through the flung-open door. "Why's the door—" she managed before she saw inside.

There, in the center of the customer area, between tall freezers and refrigerators on the right and the ice cream counter on the left, the shop's two heavy rugs were rolled into tubes. Inside the tubes were her parents. Her dad had a broad bruise over his left ear.

"Mom!" Debbie yelled. "Dad!"

"Debbie?" her mom said. She was wrapped so tight in the rug, she could barely turn her head enough to see her daughter.

"What happened?" She could feel the tears welling up inside her.

"They robbed us, Debbie," her dad said. "They robbed us. Everything in the cash register, everything in the safe—it's gone."

That money was all going toward October's house bills, Debbie knew.

"Are you okay? Mom, Dad—are you okay?" She couldn't stop looking at the ugly purple bruise above her dad's ear.

"We're fine, honey," said her mom.

"Now you get out of here, Debbie," her dad insisted. "The men just left. One of them had a gun. I don't want you near here."

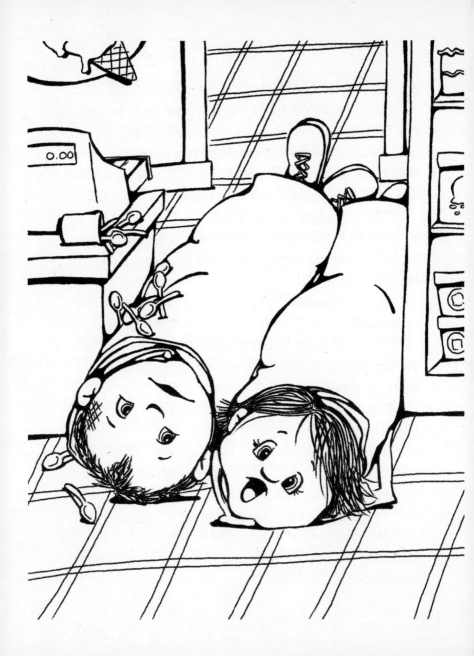

"Go somewhere and call for help," said her mom. "They cut our phone line."

Debbie didn't want to leave. "I can't leave you here," she said, tears rushing down her cheeks.

"Debbie, I need you to listen to your mother now," her father said. "Find a phone. And get yourself away from here."

Debbie turned and ran out of the shop. In some small part of her brain, a question popped: Where's T-Rex? But she didn't have time to worry about him now. Her parents were in trouble. She pushed her bike down the sidewalk and hopped onto the seat with the wheels already rolling. She rode as fast as she could around the protruding bluff to Vito's Italian Cuisine and almost jumped off her bike before seeing the closed sign. "WE WILL REOPEN FOR DINNER AT 5:30," the sign said. Debbie turned sharply and, without looking for traffic, pedaled across Main Street to Dairy Queen. Horns honked as car tires squealed and skidded to a stop. Dairy Queen's front door was open, and she rode her bike right into the restaurant.

"Call 911!" she shouted. "Call 911! Cone On In!'s been robbed! My parents have been hurt! Please help! Someone—please help!"

An employee in red rushed to the phone, and Debbie rode back out the door, turning again toward her parents' shop. She remembered, then, what her parents had said about staying away. They'd meant it too. And what could she do to help them there, anyway?

She hopped off on the sidewalk and suddenly felt as helpless as she had the day Mr. Wilson fell. Two men had gone into her parents' shop, pointed a gun at them, rolled them up in rugs, and even struck her father across his face. And there was nothing she could do about it. She hadn't been able to protect Mr. Wilson, and she certainly couldn't protect her parents. Debbie was no superhero. She looked at her bicycle and said, "Stupid bike." She kicked the front tire and then slammed the whole thing on the ground.

No, Debbie realized. *This isn't like with Mr. Wilson.* She didn't feel helpless now as she had more than a week ago, pulling on her neighbor's arms, wanting only to get him to her bike and then to the hospital. No, she didn't feel helpless now. She felt angry. Angry at the two bad men who hurt her parents. Angry at her bike too. Angry she'd ever thought she could make a difference.

Angry. Angry. Angry. Angry. Angry.

The word reminded her of something. Of an image,

first: Mr. Wilson with a scowl on his face, setting her up for his joke. What was that he'd said? Oh, yes: "Angry red bees need to fly around or they lose the ability." Days later, right before he lost consciousness, he'd said something else: "Don't forget about the angry red bees."

Each had seemed a strange comment, but today she was sure the comments were related. Two weeks ago, when she first met Mr. Wilson, she hadn't been able to make sense of that "angry red bees need to fly" part. She'd been too preoccupied with the prospect of taming angry red bees to pay much attention. Now, though— now, when it mattered most—she understood what he meant. She understood her daydream about not-flying too. Mr. Wilson, it seemed, had known more about her than she'd realized. Had he seen more that day T-Rex chased her? Had he seen her hit the curb and then, instead of splatting against the house in front of her, soar up and up? She heard the small voice inside her head again, telling her to fly, and now it was Mr. Wilson's voice. "Angry red bees need to fly around or they lose the ability," the voice said.

She picked up her shiny white Thunderstrike bicycle and kicked her leg over the seat. She knew what she had to do.

It was time to make the men who'd hurt her parents pay. They'd gone after her family, and she would protect that family. She started pedaling. "I've got to go faster," she said to herself. She pedaled a block north and then turned left—onto the town's tallest and steepest hill—a hill that began twelve blocks west of Main Street and ended at the river. Up Debbie went. Pushing hard, wobbling as she fought the hill's incline inch after inch. Debbie's legs were strong from making the trip uphill to school every day. And she didn't need to get to the top— just high enough that she could turn her bike around and build up enough speed going the other way.

When the hill became steep enough that Debbie had to fight her pedals to keep her wheels from rolling backward, she leaned hard to her left and let her bicycle tip her over. It landed on top of her, and she sprung to her feet, mounted the bike again, and let the steepness of the hill pull her down. At first she pedaled, and then she realized pedaling was worthless; the hill's incline propelled her at a clip her legs couldn't match. As she accelerated to a speed she'd never traveled before, the world screamed by, and panic flooded through her body. She remembered her daydream that afternoon, in which the sledding jump flung her wildly out but never up. She remembered that it had been more than a week since she last flew on her bicycle, and she wondered: Can I still do it?

That's when Mrs. Maple, an elderly woman who volunteered at the library, stepped out from Elegant Antique's storefront and pushed her walker to the middle of the sidewalk—no more than thirty feet from Debbie, speeding down the same sidewalk.

"Oh, no!" Debbie muttered. "Watch out!" she yelled as she pulled on the breaks hard. Her white Thunderstrike bike, traveling too fast to stop, jerked up off the ground, front wheel leading the way, swinging up and back and over. Debbie, still on her bike, flipping backwards, started to pedal. Just before the back of her head met with the sidewalk and she slid uncontrollably into the elderly woman, which would have made her responsible for two deaths that very moment, her bike was pulled vertically as if by a fishing line. She kept pedaling, and she rose up, up into the air, upside down, her head dangling down toward the ground. Reaching the tops of the buildings, she pushed on the handlebars as she pedaled, and the bike righted itself. Now she pulled gently on the handlebars and pedaled the bike up higher and higher.

Below, Mrs. Maple kept walking. She hadn't heard or seen a thing.

Debbie climbed higher.

Well above town, Debbie flew south until she was directly above her parents' shop. Three police cars and an ambulance were parked in the lot now. Seeing them and remembering anew her parents' plight and her dad's bruised face caused anger to boil within her. She would catch the criminals. She would retrieve her parents' money. She would put the bad men in jail.

A nagging question she'd been ignoring, though, couldn't be ignored any longer. How would she find the bad men?

Debbie's heart sank. She had no idea where they'd gone. Below her was a bluff dense with trees, a river that ran swiftly through and past Plaintown, and a highway that led out of town. The robbers could be anywhere. This whole ordeal, climbing the hill, flying again, trying to be a superhero—it really was all pointless. What had Mr. Wilson said about angry red bees? It hadn't meant anything. Or maybe she really would have lost the ability to fly, but it didn't matter anyway. It was just a joke, after all. Her ability to fly hadn't helped her save him, and it wasn't going to help her save her family. She'd made

Dizzy Fantastic up, as she had Diana, and there was no point hanging on to the fantasy any longer. She should just drop down the sidewalk and bike home. The bad men were gone.

She wasn't Superman, after all; she couldn't hear every voice and movement below—

But she *did* hear T-Rex's bark.

Out he pounced from the trees below to the edge of the bluff. "T-Rex!" she called. "Where have you been?" Even as she said it, she knew the answer. "You're on their scent, aren't you, boy?" That's right! He'd growled when they first got to Cone On In!, hadn't he? Before she left to call for help, her parents said the robbers had just left! Dizzy Fantastic swooped down to the bluff and hovered a few feet above T-Rex's nose. "Show me, boy," she said. "Bring me to them."

They were headed back into the trees, and Dizzy Fantastic pulled her pink-framed sunglasses from her backpack to protect her eyes from stray branches. It was the only part of her costume she had time to put on. T-Rex zigged and zagged as he followed the robbers' scent. Weaving around trees came easily to her. She recognized the feel of leaves swishing against her arms. It was just like she was back behind Plymouth Point Elementary in the grove of trees where she had trained. It was cool beneath the canopy of trees, but Dizzy Fantastic's adrenaline pumped warm sweat out of her pores. "Keep going, boy," she said. "I can follow you."

And then there in front of them ran two men dressed in camouflaged jackets and pants and black ski masks. They carried small black duffle bags slung over their shoulders that bounced around as they ran through the trees.

The bags weren't full, and it occurred to Debbie that they'd picked the wrong place to rob. Sure, they robbed Debbie's parents of all the money they had. The money in those duffels meant everything to the Fine family, but it couldn't amount to much profit for the thieves. Cone On In!, Debbie was sorry to admit, was probably the worst business to rob in town, maybe even in the country. Of course, they couldn't have known they were robbing from the parents of a fourth-grade superhero. That was just bad luck.

The men must have heard the black Lab thumping through the leaves and rocks behind them, because they turned and saw their pursuers. If they were fazed seeing a vicious dog chasing them and a fourth-grade girl on a flying bicycle, it didn't last for long. One yelled to the other, "Split up. Get out your gun."

Off they stumbled, deeper into the trees.

Dizzy Fantastic pedaled hard and zoomed through the trees until she was even with the man without a gun and ten feet above him. He was breathing heavily and looking back over his shoulder at her. She reached behind her and pulled the jar of peanut butter from her backpack. She unscrewed the top and scooped up a gob of chunky peanut butter. She said, "I feel bad for you" as she turned her palm down and let the gob of peanut butter fall on the man's head. Still running, he patted the top of his head with his hand, pressing the peanut butter down and spreading it on top of his ski mask. "What in the world . . . ?" he muttered, looking at his now-sticky hand and not understanding.

T-Rex, seeing the peanut butter, leapt forward, picking up his pace. Just in front of a tree she was speeding toward, Dizzy Fantastic turned her handlebars and sped after the other man—the man with the gun. She weaved through trees, rising up and dipping down to avoid branches.

Dizzy Fantastic spotted the man in camouflage ahead, running forward and shooting wildly behind him.

Hot on his trail, steering her bike with one hand, she reached back with the other into her backpack and took out a rock left over from her training session behind the school.

A gunshot punctured the air. The bullet whistled by her and burrowed through a tree trunk. In her sudden turn to avoid the startling sound of the bullet—she'd never been shot at before!—her back wheel smacked a tree. Her bike bounced violently off the trunk, nearly tipping, and threatened to buck Debbie off.

With a rock in her right hand, she had only her left hand to steer. She leaned to the left, pedaled hard, and turned her bike sharply. After spinning in a tight circle, she righted herself, and another bullet hissed by her.

Debbie gulped back fear.

She took a deep breath, tightened her grip on the left handlebar, and moved the rock in her palm to her fingers. She whipped around a tree, lowering her face for protection as she plowed through leafy branches, and, looking up, cleared herself for a throw. The man with the gun stumbled in front of her. She chucked the rock with all she had at the running robber. It missed him and settled on the damp leaves below.

Swerving around another tree, she reached back again and grabbed another rock. She dipped under a branch and, as the man ran between two trees fifteen yards in front of her, pelted him in the head. To her surprise, he fell to the ground and the gun flew out of his hand! She dove close to him. As he tried to get up, she threw four more rocks and two walnuts. They hit the man's shoulder blades and the back of his neck, pushing and pinning him to the ground.

She stopped pedaling, pulled her legs up, and stood on the seat, letting her white Thunderstrike bicycle drop down on top of the man, who grunted as the tires pounded his body into the leaves and dirt. As the bike listed, she jumped off and landed on her feet.

"Who—?" he coughed.

"Dizzy Fantastic, fourth-grade superhero, and you've made a big mistake, harming good people in this town." She wiped her sweaty face with her dirty sweatshirt sleeve.

She threw one more walnut, this one at the man's head, and knocked him out.

That's when she heard leaves rustling behind her— another bad guy?—Debbie reached back for something to throw when T-Rex came padding up to her, a small duffle that smelled of peanut butter dangling from his mouth.

·.★THIRTY-ONE★·:

All the money was still in the duffels," Debbie's dad said as the Fine family ate Good Dinner. His wife had secured a bag of ice over his right ear with plastic wrap. "The police found them behind our parking lot. The robbers must have dropped them as they ran away."

"Did they get away, Dad?" James asked.

"No—it appears somebody else got to them, but we don't know who. The police found them beat up in the woods. They're in the hospital now, recovering. One had welts all over and bicycle tire tracks up and down his backside. The other's clothes were chewed up. His face was bit up pretty bad by some kind of animal. It was like a lion had mauled him." As she had weeks before, when T-Rex chased her down the hill, Debbie thought about the video the substitute teacher had shown of a lion tackling and devouring a gazelle. This time, the thought brought a grin to her face.

"Your sister is the hero, James," her mother said. "She

raced over to Dairy Queen and had them call the police. She must be getting pretty fast on that bike."

James nodded. "Way to go, Debbie."

"You know what else, James? Today I stood on the seat." She thought of her bike's wheels digging into the bad man's back, and she couldn't help that her grin expanded.

Her brother smiled. "Nice. Usually girls won't do that one."

"I'm just grateful Debbie came down to the shop today," her dad said.

"Family's the only thing any of us truly needs, right Dad?" said Debbie.

"Right."

Debbie nudged T-Rex with her toe. He was sleeping under the table.

★·★·★·

Before going to bed, Debbie shoved her half-painted Barbie house and all of her dolls into the back of her closet. She would take it out again sometime, she was sure, and finish painting the ballroom, but for now she had too many real people to worry about.

Dizzy Fantastic would be busy, she knew.

★·★THIRTY-TWO★·★

The next day, school was abuzz with news of another sighting of the fourth-grade superhero. Students up and down the halls held newspapers open and wondered aloud who it could be. Wendell Washington reported that she'd beaten up two would-be thieves. According to one of the thieves, Dizzy Fantastic now had a slobbering dog for a sidekick. "Does this flying girl really go to our school?" Plymouth Point students wondered. "Does she really fly on a bicycle?"

Debbie spotted Davey standing with three other boys in their class. She tapped him on the shoulder. "I need a favor," she said.

"Well, okay."

"My family—we can't afford to take care of T-Rex. He's too big, and he eats too much, and we're poor. My parents won't admit that we can't take care of him, because they feel bad about Mr. Wilson and all, but it's true. So I guess I'm asking if you'd be willing take him."

Davey nodded his head. "Sure. I'll take him. Well—I need to ask my mom, but I'm sure she'll say it's okay."

"Really? That'd be great. Thanks, Davey." She turned to leave, but couldn't. She tapped him on the shoulder again.

"Something else?"

"Can I borrow him sometimes?"

"T-Rex? Of course."

She threw her arms around him. The boy wearing sweatpants, a basketball jersey down to his knees, and a bowl cut, didn't know what to do, so he hugged her back.

★·:★.★·:

When she left Davey, Debbie didn't go to class right away. She fought her way through the crowded hallways, using both hands to brush aside the newspapers held up by students. It was like brushing aside tall grass on a safari. She was in a hurry. The first bell of the day would ring soon, and she had something she needed to say before it did.

★·:★.★·:

Tabby's door, as always, was open a crack. Debbie knocked.

"Push it open," came the familiar response.

Debbie did, and Tabby smiled as she entered. The counselor was wearing a long yellow dress and yellow hoop earrings. Her gold necklace and rings glittered. She had the newspaper open in front of her. "Miss Debbie, we don't meet until tomorrow afternoon—or did Principal Paulsen change your schedule?"

"No, it wasn't changed, but—but I wanted to thank you for all your help and I couldn't wait." She said this quickly as she breathed short shallow breaths, still recovering from making her way hurriedly through the halls.

"Why—how thoughtful. And of course you're welcome."

Debbie nodded and shrugged at the same time. And then she froze. Suddenly Debbie wasn't sure she wanted to say what she'd come to say. She turned and took a step through the door and out of Tabbyville.

The counselor's voice called her back. "Hey, Debbie— it looked for a moment like you had something else on your mind. Is that right? Is there anything I can do for you right now?"

Debbie took a deep breath, pulled her foot back even with the other, and pivoted so she was looking again at the counselor. "I guess I wanted to ask you a question too," she muttered.

"What is it, Debbie Fine?"

Debbie took another deep breath. "I was wondering if—if sometimes you—just you—would call me Dizzy Fantastic?"

Still smiling, the counselor crinkled her nose and looked down at the newspaper on her desk. Wendell Washington's article was on the front page. She stared at it for a few seconds. Then Tabby glanced back up and sized up the girl in front of her. Her smile widened. "I can certainly do that," she said.

About the Author

★ ⁙ ★ ⁙

This picture was taken when Andy Hueller was five years old. He holds in his hands the first book he ever wrote. He's very proud. It's written in ITA, a beginning-English language. He often wears a bed-sheet cape around the house, and he takes part in secret superhero meetings with his twin brother and their older sister. They meet behind hanging clothes in the playroom closet and decide how they will defeat the bad guys and protect the good guys.

Now, over twenty years later, you hold in your hands Mr. Hueller's first published novel. He's proud of this book too. His writing goals haven't changed since he was five. He wants readers to learn and be happy.

Mr. Hueller lives in Minneapolis, Minnesota, with his fantastic wife. He teaches at St. Paul Academy and Summit School.